by a Supervillain
Supervillain Romance Project #3

H. L. Burke

For information about H. L. Burke's latest novels, to sign up for the author's newsletter, or to contact the author, go to www.hlburkeauthor.com

Free eBook for Newsletter Subscribers!

Copyright © 2022 H. L. Burke
All rights reserved.
Cover art by K. M. Carroll
Cover layout by Jennifer Hudzinski

To Lady Kaz Cat. Welcome to the family.
—Heidi

Chapter One

Juliet Park, AKA Zest, soared above the city, occasionally checking the read-out on the smartphone strapped to her forearm. The Department of Super-Abled had provided her team with an app that would alert them to anomalous energy signatures and blips in the power grid. She'd been circling the section her team had assigned her for what felt like hours, though, and nothing had shown up. There had to be a faster way to find supervillains so she could get to the actual fighting.

She slowed her flight to a hover and adjusted her goggles. Most flying type sables—short for super-abled—didn't bother with eye protection, but Juliet liked to push her flying to max speed. Not now, of course. Now she was supposed to fly in leisurely circles, observing the area around her. Superheroing could be super boring sometimes.

Her stomach grumbled, and her thoughts turned to the burrito bowl she had carefully wrapped in her backpack. She wanted to stop and eat so much, but her team leader—Pangolin, a man with the ability to transform his skin into armored plates—had told her she needed to keep patrolling until her shift was over. According to her phone, that was still two hours away.

She turned in a slow circle, examining bustling streets, tall buildings, and pedestrians, none of whom paid any attention to her. It was understandable. Heroes were everywhere these days with DOSA having teams in most mid-sized to large cities. The big ones with impressive deeds under their belts might gain a following, but Juliet—at only twenty-three—wasn't much of a name yet. The most she'd ever gotten was an, "Oh, my, are you Verve's daughter? He was my favorite hero growing up! So inspiring, the first Korean American DOSA hero."

As much as she loved her dad, the shadow of her family legacy—well, it kind of sucked.

A flash of bright blue caught her eye. A city bus? Perfect!

Zipping her black and purple motorcycle jacket up to her chin, she kicked her boots together and dove for the bus. She slowed and rotated to glide above it for a moment then gently landed on the roof, right in the center. If she kept low, no one would see her sitting there and the movement of the bus would satisfy Pangolin's requirements just enough that she could eat her burrito bowl in peace.

Removing her backpack, she settled cross-legged and fished out her lunch. As she opened the container, she closed her eyes to savor the smell of grilled chicken in Adobo sauce before opening them and having her heart sink.

"Crap! I said no cheese!" Grumbling to herself, she picked pieces of shredded yellow dairy product off the top of her otherwise perfect burrito bowl. Lactose intolerance was a curse even superpowers couldn't mitigate. Finally convinced she'd gotten most of it, she dug in only to have her phone go off.

She grunted, praying it wasn't Pangolin, and checked the readout.

"Call from Shawn-Bawn."

She needed to change her brother's contact name to something less embarrassing. Pushing her goggles up into her shiny black hair, she answered, "Roadkill Cafe, you kill 'em, we grill 'em. Are you interested in today's mystery meat special?"

There was a brief pause then an exaggerated sigh. "Good to see you remain untouched by age or maturity."

"Hey, we can't all be responsible suburban dads." She took a big bite of beans and rice. "Speaking of which, how's the brood? Any sign of powers yet?"

"Only if you count being super-humanly adorable, but that's kind of why I'm calling," Shawn said. "Wanted you to know before it hits Instagram later today: Katie's pregnant."

Juliet choked, sending rice spraying. "Again? Already?"

"I mean, we took a little bit of a break. Hana's almost two."

"I guess. You're aiming for a full house, aren't you?"

"We're gonna call it after this one. I'm kind of hoping this is a boy just so I'm not completely outnumbered, but even if it's not, three's my limit—probably."

"*Probably.*" Juliet then allowed her voice to soften. "I'm happy for you. If this one is anything like Hana and Evie, she's going to be a doll."

"Already assuming it'll be a she, huh?" Shawn asked.

"You're not that lucky, brother boy. You wanting a boy means this baby's gonna come out wearing pink and wrapping you around her little finger."

"You're probably right. I'm not complaining. I wouldn't trade my girls for the world." The line went silent. Juliet resumed her snacking, quietly musing on the excitement of a new Park baby and all the ways she could use it to tease her brother.

"Oh, did you have a chance to read that book I sent you?" Shawn asked.

She swallowed. "Uh, yeah. It's ... it's interesting."

About a year before, Shawn's mother-in-law had started taking their daughters to Sunday school and after that, Shawn had gotten—weird. Apparently Katie was really into her mother's faith and the girls were excited about it, and her brother, being the type to be into things his loved ones were into, had gone all-in shortly after.

"Interesting, huh? You wanna talk about it?"

"I guess there's nothing wrong with the ideas. I can see why you like them," she chose her words carefully.

"I see them as a little more than 'ideas.'" He laughed quietly.

"And that's great, but for me .... I need more to believe in something than a cool concept. Like you know, solid proof?" She took another bite.

"Proof? You mean like a sign from heaven?"

"Sure. Or a miracle. You believe in those right." Her mouth curled into a grin. She had him there.

"Oh, I do, but it's a big ask to order one up like I'm getting a pizza. Anyway, that's my news and my brotherly nagging. How's everything with you?"

"Good." The bus slowed beneath her, and a car honked. She needed to get moving, especially because she knew what Shawn wanted to talk about, and she didn't want to.

"Even with what happened last month? All of DOSA's on edge about it, and it was your city. That's got to be hard on your team."

Juliet grimaced. "I mean, villain attacks happen. This one came out of nowhere. There was nothing we could've done to predict it or stop it."

"Doesn't mean it's not hard," Shawn pointed out.

"Yeah, but ... I don't know. I hate how pointless it

was," Juliet said. "Six people died in that explosion, and for what? From what we can tell the villains didn't get anything out of it. They didn't make any demands. They just blew up a building for no dang reason."

"Villains are villains, Jules," Shawn said. "Has anyone taken credit yet, though?"

"Sort of—" She hesitated. If Shawn didn't know, DOSA might be holding back the information. That said, she hadn't been told not to talk about it internally. With the press, of course not. She wasn't an idiot, but Shawn was both family and DOSA. "We think it might be a Black Fox cell."

"Really?" Intrigue flavored Shawn's voice. "That far north?"

"Yeah, they haven't been active in this area before, but Pangolin compared some notes with other regional team leaders, and what limited CCTV footage we got of the team matches with three of their known agents: Diamondback, Sandstorm, and Mentallica."

"Great. I thought we'd finally eradicated that cancer." Shawn huffed.

"They had too many splinter groups stationed around the country. Yeah, we've been good about smashing down the larger ones, but you know what Mom used to say about weeding? If you don't get the roots, it always comes back next year." Juliet pulled a water bottle from her pack and took a swig. She still had most of her burrito bowl left, but this conversation was sapping her appetite. She needed to get serious about patrol, even if it was boring. "We can't go back in time and stop them, but at least we can prevent it from happening again—and hopefully bring them in and make them pay for it."

"That's the job. Just remember, if you need to talk about it. I'm here."

"There's nothing to talk about. Pangolin's got the team on edge, watching out for any sign of another attack, but we've got it covered." Giving up on lunch, she wrapped up her leftovers and shoved them into her backpack again. "Speaking of which, though, I need to get back on patrol."

"By the way, there's a lot of background noise there—where are you?"

"On the bus." Juliet bit back a laugh.

"Inside or outside?"

"What are you? My dad?"

"Jeez, Jules. You know DOSA had break rooms, right?"

"Got to go, Big Bro. Say hi to Katie and the girls for me." She hopped up and shouldered her backpack.

"Yeah, I will. Love you."

"You too." She hung up and pushed off into the air. A horn blared as she rose above the traffic, and she threw a thumbs-up at the nearby cars before swooping over the rooftops to continue her quest.

In spite of her renewed determination to capture the villains, after two more slow circuits around her assigned area, she began checking the time again. There had to be a more efficient way of doing this.

For Juliet, slow flying took about the same energy as a leisurely stroll—but Juliet never bothered with "slow" anything. After several hours of what amounted to a continued jog with short sprints, though, her muscles started to ache. She landed on a ledge for a breather. She closed her eyes. It was mid-September and unseasonably cold. As soon as she stopped moving the crisp fall breeze found her and she shivered.

How much longer did she have to do this? Pangolin really didn't expect his team to keep running in circles on the off chance the villains showed up, did he? Of course, for the others that meant riding in cars or occasionally helicopters. Juliet was the only one on her team who could actually fly.

"This is never going to work."

Her phone buzzed loudly against her forearm.

Juliet jumped, wobbled, and activated her powers, catching herself from falling by bursting into the air once more. She checked the phone.

Energy anomaly detected.

Her breath quickened. It was less than two blocks from her current location.

She tapped her ear, activating the earpiece connected to her team's communication channel.

"Team, this is Zest. The scanner caught something near my location. Do you have the coordinates?"

"We've got it," Pangolin's gravelly voice came over the channel. "Weak signal, though. Could be a false alarm. We're headed towards you, just in case, but see if you can get eyes on the area. If you see anything, be cautious. Don't engage until we're at your location."

"Roger." Juliet fastened her goggles in place, preparing for a quick burst of speed, then zoomed towards the site. Her location merged with the pulsing dot on the map over what appeared to be a generic apartment building, an older brick structure, maybe about five stories. She settled on the roof of the taller building next to it so she could get a bird's eye view while maintaining some cover.

A delivery van idled out front. Potentially suspicious but could also be someone getting their Amazon packages. Some civilians walking around and ... one guy on the roof. What was he doing?

She narrowed her eyes at him before turning a small dial on the side of her goggles, magnifying her vision. A tall man with dusty brown hair stood in the middle of the roof. He wore what looked to be jeans and a black jacket and was turning in a slow circle, something silver clasped in his extended hand.

Juliet hesitated. They weren't sure exactly what caused the energy bursts that had book-ended the previous attack. They only knew that the power grid had registered surges shortly before and immediately after the explosion that had destroyed an office building and killed several civilians. Could whatever this man was holding be the cause? He didn't appear to be otherwise armed, though that often didn't matter with supervillains.

As she watched the man's whole body shimmered, growing transparent. He drew his arms close to his body and melted through the roof beneath his feet, like a rabbit disappearing down a burrow. Juliet's jaw dropped.

"We've got a sable." Her brain scrambled. She hadn't seen the attackers last time and the CCTV footage had been blurry, but one of their numbers, Sandstorm, was a matter manipulator. That had to be him. "I think it's Sandstorm. He just went through the roof."

"Crap!" Pangolin cursed.

"Is he alone? Did you see the other two?" Kesia, also known as Klaxon, chimed in.

"I don't see any—" Juliet rose into the air, trying to get eyes on the alleyways on either side of the building. Her throat tightened when she noticed several balconies off the various apartments with toys on them, even a stroller on one. Families lived in this building. If there was another bomb—

"We need to call for an evacuation!" she said. "There could be dozens of people in there."

"Maybe hundreds," Donny, the team's strength sable, piped in over the line. "What should we do, boss?"

"I think I should—" Juliet began, only to be cut off by Pangolin.

"We've got first responders en route. Don't be—"

It was an even chance whether the next word out of Pangolin's mouth would be "reckless" or "stupid" but either way, it didn't matter. Juliet hit mute and dove for the building. She had an idea.

She zoomed down and scanned the outside of the building. An open balcony door on the third story caught her eye, and she aimed for it.

A small dog barked frantically as she landed beside him.

"Edna, what's going on, sweetie?" an elderly voice called out. "Is it the pigeons again—"

An old woman stepped into view and her jaw dropped.

"Uh, sorry, ma'am. DOSA emergency. Please grab your dog and get outside." Juliet hurried past the gaping woman and into the hallway outside the apartment, scanning the walls.

There!

She rushed for the fire alarm and threw the switch. Bells clamored and clanged. A few apartment doors opened and people stumbled out. Hopefully, most of them didn't think it was some sort of drill.

"Clear out! Clear out! DOSA emergency," Juliet shouted.

She wondered if she should reactivate her comm. Checking in with her team was smart, but she'd already disobeyed orders, and getting yelled at would be a distraction she didn't need right now.

Her goal completed, she hustled towards the nearest exit, following a couple of confused residents including the old woman and the still barking dog. Her mother had always been strict about no flying in the house, and as much as she wanted to zip down the hall, she might knock over a slow-moving normie if she tried it in this narrow space.

Juliet entered the stairwell. Now to fly.

As she made the second bend, something black caught her eye, melting through the floor again.

Sandstorm!

He seemed to be alone and unaware of her pursuit. She quickened her pace, going past the lobby exit and down into the basement level just in time to see the villain break into a cloud of particles and slip under the door. Juliet hesitated. Was she really going to confront him on her own?

Creeping closer, she peeked through the window in the door. Fluorescent lights flickered in the space beyond, but she couldn't see him. Any other villain would be cornered, but Sandstorm was different. His power set made him practically uncontainable. If she hesitated, he'd get away. She reached into her pocket for a disrupter cuff. If she could get it on him, his powers would short-circuit, and he'd be stuck.

It's worth a try.

She eased the door open. The space beyond was filled with storage containers and old junk. Probably a fire hazard. She kept to the wall, listening for any sign of him. One of the storage pods was open. She swallowed. He had to be in there. Hovering off the floor to avoid footsteps, she glided closer. Yep, sure enough, he crouched over something in the corner of the mostly empty storage container. Something square and ...

Oh, gosh, that's a bomb! He's setting a bomb.

Juliet threw her hands forward, sending all her power into her palms and fingertips until it hummed about her like a reverberating speaker. It shot out of her as Sandstorm faced her. He fragmented again, but too late. Her blast hit him, and he collided with the back of the container, wheezing.

She hit her earpiece. "I've got Sandstorm in the basement. He's got a bomb. Get an EOD team down here fast!"

"Park, what are you doing?" Pangolin's scream made her ears ring.

Before she could respond, Sandstorm picked himself up and rubbed his back. "Oof, you hit hard for your weight class. Sorry I can't stick around." His body wavered like a mirage on a hot day.

Juliet rushed forward, disruptor in hand, determined to get it on him, but her hand went right through his body. He snickered and stepped through her. For a moment his body and hers occupied the same space. A weird, tingling energy so unlike that of her own powers shivered through her like static. She gasped and pulled away, twisting around to find him between her and the door.

"Give my regards to DOSA." He winked.

Her teeth gritted together, and she threw another power blast. His particles wavered, and he stumbled back a step. He snapped solid for a second. She lashed out with the cuff which when unfastened took the form of a flexible rod. He dodged, spun, and caught her wrist in his hand.

"Nope. Not happening." His hazel eyes locked with hers. A shiver cut through her. Dang, it was hard to be a hero when her type was bad boys. The guy had nice eyes. She forced herself to sneer at him.

"Jules, what's going on? We're almost there." This time it was Kesia in her ear.

Footsteps clattered in the stairwell accompanied by shouting.

Sandstorm's jaw clenched, and he shoved Juliet away. She stumbled backwards, hitting the wall of the storage unit with a clang.

"You're trapped!" she said. "Just give up, and we'll go easy on you."

"I'm a hard guy to pin down." He reached into his pocket and withdrew the silver disk she'd seen him holding on the roof. Her heart stilled. Was it the detonator? Was he about to blow them *both* up?

Light sprang from the disk, creating a glowing blue circle beside Sandstorm. The lights in the building flickered then went out.

"See you later, short stuff." Sandstorm took a step towards the light.

Oh, no, you don't!

Juliet sprang forward and grabbed him by the arm only to have him stumble through the wall of light, pulling her along with him. The light blinded her and energy crackled around her, making her hair stand on end.

"Crap! Let go!" He pried her fingers off his arm as the light dissipated. Juliet blinked. Concrete walls surrounded them in a windowless room lit by lights built into the ceiling. They weren't in the basement anymore. Portable teleportation tech? How was that even possible?

She whirled around. The portal was gone.

Chapter Two

Juliet reeled as she took in their new surroundings.

"Crap, crap, crap," Sandstorm muttered. He fiddled with the disk then flung it away in frustration. "And of course, it's burned out."

"How—how did we get here?" she stammered.

Voices called out. "Lucas, you idiot. Where've you been?"

The door across the room opened, and two people entered, a youngish white guy with reddish-brown hair and a black woman who looked to be also in her early twenties. Come to think of it, Sandstorm himself didn't appear to be any older than Juliet was. This was a young team. The man wore olive fatigues, but the woman just had on jeans and a T-shirt with a cartoon brain in a jar on it.

"What the—" The woman's eyes widened.

Juliet threw out her hands, ready to blast them both. Sandstorm tackled her. His arms surrounded her, pinning her hands behind her back and preventing her from getting a shot off. He snatched the disruptor cuff from her and slapped it around her wrists. Juliet cried out as her powers disappeared like a match blown out.

"I needed to check on one of the devices." He released her with a push that sent her to her knees. He plucked the earpiece from her ear and tossed it onto the tile floor, crushing it with the heel of his work boot.

Juliet's head spun. This couldn't be happening. She'd sworn she had everything under control. How had she been so stupid?

"I was getting weird readouts from it. There was a chance it might go off prematurely," Sandstorm continued. "I got made. It won't happen again."

"Is he telling the truth, Mentallica?" a calm, feminine voice asked. Everyone looked to the doorway as a woman of about fifty in a gray blazer and pencil skirt strode in. She eyed the younger woman.

Mentallica shrugged. "Seems to be, boss."

The boss faced Sandstorm. "Would it have been such a bad thing for one of the devices to go off a few weeks early? We could call it another warning shot. The timing issue on the first bomb meant it didn't produce nearly the effect I wanted."

"You know how DOSA works. They're already on high alert, but if there's a second attack on the same city within a short period? They're gonna lock it down. At that point, high chance they'll start finding more devices or evacuating sections of the city. It'll make it harder to pull off the plan when the time is right." Sandstorm rolled his shoulders so that his jacket fell a little more naturally. While young, he was the tallest person in the room by several inches, a couple of inches over six feet.

The boss nodded slowly. "And the girl?"

"She ... kind of came along for the ride." Sandstorm laughed awkwardly.

Juliet picked herself up off the floor. "My team will have found your device by now. It's gone. We stopped you —"

"It's one of five." The boss gave a cold smile.

Juliet's heart dropped into her stomach. She'd gotten herself captured and accomplished ... so little. She kind of wanted to cry.

"What do we do with her?" Mentallica asked.

"I have some ideas." The other man stepped forward, leering at her. Juliet tensed. Sandstorm moved between her and his teammate.

"Ew, Diamondback, don't be gross." Mentallica shoved him.

"Yes, none of that," the boss woman said. "That said,

we're at a crucial point in this mission. The DOSA agent is a wildcard we can't afford." She nodded to Sandstorm. "You brought her here. You deal with her. Don't make a mess. Quick and clean. We're in this for business, not pleasure."

Cold rushed through Juliet. She staggered to her feet, but without her powers and with the cuff holding her hands behind her back, she didn't have a chance against one supervillain, let alone four. Prayers and promises from her brother's dang book rushed through her head in a jumbled mess. What she wouldn't do for a miracle right now.

Sandstorm's hands formed into fists. She cringed. He wasn't going to try and do this with his bare hands, was he? That seemed like an excruciating way to go. Not wanting to give them the satisfaction of seeing her afraid —even if she was terrified—she squared her shoulders.

"Go for it. Kill a bound woman like a coward," she spat. "I wouldn't expect more from Black Fox scum."

"Yeah, Sandstorm, do it," Diamondback taunted. "What are you waiting for? Don't have the guts?"

Sandstorm cut Diamondback an irritated look then shook his head. "This is shortsighted. We're not thinking strategically."

"How so?" The boss tilted her head to one side.

"She's a hostage. She's valuable. We can make use of her. Also, locking her up for a day or two won't hurt the mission." He turned to face his team. "It's not like DOSA can track her here. We made sure of that."

"He's squeamish. I'll do it if he won't, boss. I'm not afraid to get my hands dirty—or my mouth." Diamondback's smile broadened to reveal a pair of snake-like fangs. Juliet didn't know whether to scream, laugh, or gag.

"Wallace, who's better at dealing with DOSA? Me or Huxley?" Sandstorm jerked his thumb at Diamondback.

"What's that supposed to mean?" Diamondback

snarled.

"I mean there's a reason your brother wanted to recruit me before him," Sandstorm kept his eyes on the boss—Wallace apparently. "DOSA's been picking off our cells for the last several years. They sniped Huxley's team right out from under him. Ours stayed intact through the worst of it. Why? Because you've always listened to me, and you know it."

Huxley's face went crimson. "That's bull—"

"He's right," Wallace interrupted. "Sandstorm knows how DOSA works. That said, I'm still not sold. You come up with a plan to make having her as a prisoner work for us, and she stays. If not, she goes. We'll take no drastic action—yet." She eyed Juliet who did her best to keep her face expressionless.

Easy, she told herself. *Not out of the woods yet, but at least not going to get immediately un-alived.*

"In the meantime, we need to reassess. We can assume DOSA found the device you were working on, and chances are they'll be looking for more." Wallace brushed a stray gray hair that had escaped her otherwise pristine French twist hairstyle. "Since the girl is your prisoner, you're in charge of making sure she's secure. Search her well. If she has any sort of tracking device on her, destroy it."

Sandstorm shifted from foot to foot. "Uh, maybe Mentallica—"

"Oh, I'll help!" Diamondback volunteered.

Mentallica put out her hand, and Diamondback staggered back, gripping his temples.

"Crap! What was that for?"

"You're creeping me out," Mentallica said simply.

"Diamondback, I want you to check the readings for the remaining devices," Wallace said calmly. "If one was malfunctioning, the others might be. If one goes off early, it's inconvenient. If they all do, we'll lose our leverage."

"Yes, ma'am," Diamondback said through gritted

teeth.

He left followed by a silent Wallace.

"Thanks," Juliet murmured as Mentallica approached her.

"Don't." The woman's face hardened. "As far as I'm concerned, you're only alive because Sandstorm thinks you might have value. We're not gonna be friends."

Dang, Juliet couldn't help if her mom had raised her to be polite. She eyed Sandstorm who turned away as Mentallica patted her down.

"I need to take her jacket and backpack off." Mentallica pulled at the disruptor cuff that made this impossible. "Can you get me a controller?"

"Sure." Sandstorm walked to a series of drawers on the wall and pushed several buttons, probably entering a keycode. One of the doors slid open, and he reached in and took out a small device that looked a bit like a car's key fob. While disruptors were originally DOSA tech, it wasn't too hard to buy them on the black market, and all of them used essentially the same controllers.

Juliet perked up. Maybe this was her chance. If they took the disruptor off...

Sandstorm reached into an inner pocket of his jacket and pulled out another disruptor cuff. She deflated.

"Get her boots off first," Sandstorm said.

"Or I could just—" Mentallica grabbed Juliet in a Vulcan-neck-pinch-like hold. A jolt of weird, numbing energy went through Juliet then all went black.

***

Sandstorm leaped forward and caught the DOSA agent as she slumped. "Did you have to do that?"

Mentallica waved dismissively. "It'll be a lot easier for us to deal with her if she's unconscious. Help me get her boots off."

Sandstorm carefully lowered the woman to the floor as Mentallica unlaced her black boots covered in a pattern of purple constellations.

"She's got good taste." Mentallica held up the boot. "Unfortunately they're too small for me."

"Double check them for tracking devices," Sandstorm ordered, using the controller to release the disruptor cuff from her wrists. He moved the cuff to her now bootless ankle and redid it.

He slipped her phone out of her armband and examined it. No signal so DOSA couldn't have tracked her. The screen was locked so he held up her hand and pressed her fingertip to the pad. It unlocked, and he started going through her contacts. He needed to find something they could use if he wanted to get Wallace on his side.

Or, you know, you could just not be a wuss and kill her, Mentallica's voice echoed in his brain.

His powers flared, pushing her out of his thoughts. "You know I hate that." He shook his head like a dog trying to get water out of his ears.

"Yeah, but you know Wallace likes me to peek into y'all's brains when you're being weird." Mentallica slipped off the agent's backpack and unzipped it. She pulled out a to-go container of food, opened it, sniffed it, then set it aside. "You're definitely acting weird."

"Because I don't want to kill a girl in cold blood?" He snorted.

"We've all got worse on our hands," Mentallica muttered, prying off the hero's jacket and going through her pockets. Beneath the jacket, the agent wore a light gray tank top.

Sandstorm averted his eyes as his teammate continued her pat down, instead focusing on the phone. He tried her Instagram, and he gave out a low whistle when he saw her username. "Crap, she's a DOSA princess."

"A what?" Mentallica asked.

He showed her the screen. "We've got Zest, otherwise known as Juliet Park, youngest daughter of Verve, longtime leader of DOSA's Columbus branch. She's a legacy sable."

"So?" Mentallica rolled her eyes. "It's not like DOSA pays enough that her family will be able to ransom her and you know DOSA's position about negotiating with villains. They won't give us anything to get her back. Whoever she is, she's still useless."

"Maybe not—" Sandstorm murmured going back to her photos. He paused on an image of her side-hugging a somewhat older man, late twenties, probably. The guy had her same black hair, brown eyes, and high cheekbones. "I think this is her brother. Surge, maybe? He's an up-and-coming DOSA star." He looked from Juliet to Mentallica. "DOSA won't pay to get her back and her family might not have money, but he might bend the rules to keep her safe."

Mentallica's brow furrowed. "You're saying we extort him with her?"

"I'm saying Wallace won't turn down having a DOSA agent in her back pocket. Especially now with the mission at a critical point. If he can report on their investigation to us, we can stay a step ahead of them."

"Maybe—" she said slowly.

Juliet moaned.

"Sleep's wearing off. Where are we going to keep her?" Mentallica asked.

He went over the bunker in his head. "My quarters have a bathroom and a door we can lock easily from the outside. Should be secure."

Mentallica scrutinized him. "Your quarters, huh?"

"I'm not Diamondback," he said.

"Most men claim they're not. Doesn't mean they won't act like him if they get half a chance."

"I have a feeling you've been in my brain enough to know exactly what I'm like," he scoffed. "No one hides anything from you."

"You do, but I don't think it's that you're a creep." She

nodded towards the door. "Don't suppose you need help carrying her?"

"Nah, I got it." Sandstorm hoisted Juliet up as Mentallica gathered her scattered personal effects.

The sleeping quarters for the team were past the command center and down an elevator to the lower level. By the time Sandstorm reached the elevator, she was already stirring. As the doors slid open, and he stepped into the enclosed space, her eyes popped open. She gave a muffled squeal and swung out at him. Instinctively, his powers activated. Her hands passed harmlessly through his fragmented face. He managed to keep his arms solid so he didn't drop her, but she squirmed so much that he set her down. She stumbled into the corner and braced herself against the wall, glowering at him.

"You're feisty," he commented.

"Don't touch me." Her hands strayed to her now bare arms, and guilt flooded through him. She had to feel so vulnerable right now. He opened his mouth to say something comforting but remembered that pretty much the entire facility was in Mentallica's range. She might not be actively watching him at the moment, but with her recent expression of suspicion, he couldn't risk showing weakness. Not with the whole mission on a knife's edge and Diamondback already out for blood. Still, it wouldn't do to have the prisoner scuffling with him in the elevator. He needed to de-escalate the situation.

"No one is going to hurt you. You're a valuable prisoner."

Her mouth twisted.

The elevator doors closed, and her eyes flitted to them like a caged animal. He groaned inwardly. She was making it very hard to control his thoughts. Thankfully the elevator ride was quick. The doors opened, and he waved to the corridor they revealed. "Ladies first."

She wrinkled her nose at him.

"Okay, short stuff, let me make this clear. With your

powers, you might have a chance against me. A slim one, but a chance. With that cuff on your ankle—" He nodded towards it. "Well, let's just say, I've got you by a foot in height and at least a hundred pounds in body weight, and I'm fine using either to my advantage. So I repeat, ladies first."

She hesitated then peeled herself off the wall and pushed by him. "Whatever, Sandy."

"Never heard that one before," he muttered as he followed her out.

His door was the second from the elevator, the first belonging to a small storage room they kept secure with a padlock. When he opened his door, she eyed him suspiciously.

"It's just someplace you can stay for now," he explained. "We aren't exactly set up for guests."

"Is that what you're calling me? Your guest?"

"Guest, prisoner, hostage, name doesn't matter. What matters is you'll have some privacy and a comfortable place to sleep. Plus won't have to keep you tied up or whatever." He waved her forward.

Her shoulders slumped, but she stepped into the room and did a slow turn about it.

Sandstorm cleared his throat and picked up a worn backpack from the floor. Villain life kept him on the move, and he rarely unpacked between hideouts. He grabbed a few scattered clothing items from the floor and shoved them into the pack.

"This is your room?" she asked.

"Uh, yeah." His hand strayed to his jacket pocket where a smooth metal disk—a worn bottle cap—rested. He fingered it anxiously before turning to face her again. "Don't worry, though. You'll have it to yourself. I'll bunk down elsewhere."

"Huh." She stood in awkward silence, watching him, as he gathered his personal effects from the bathroom. He managed to get his spare pair of shoes and his toiletries into the pack. A set of weights sat next to the bed and he had some reading material stashed away—he could get all that later. It wasn't like he'd need it tonight.

"You know DOSA's probably already tracking me and on their way here," she said when he put his hand on the door to leave. "You want any chance of getting out of this without the fight of your life, you should let me go then take off in the opposite direction. You all leave now, you might escape before every DOSA agent in a hundred miles swarms this dump."

A smile crossed his face. "Nice try."

Her face reddened. "I'm serious."

"Yeah, and so am I. As bluffs go, that wasn't half bad." He leaned against the door. "First off, DOSA doesn't plant trackers on their people unless they're going undercover. They mostly rely on cell phones for check-ins since they're more reliable and have better range than most tracking tech. Second, this facility blocks phone signals, so as soon as you ported in with me, they lost that connection. They have no idea where you are."

Her eyes misted up. His skin crawled, and he prayed she wouldn't start crying. Today was already enough of a crap show without having to deal with that.

"Look, I didn't intend to bring you here, but I've set things up so that you're safe for now," he said quickly. "Stay quiet, be smart, and you might get through this."

"Forgive me if I'm not counting on 'be nice to the supervillains' as a great survival strategy." She backed away from him, stopping right at his unmade bed. "Your group blew up a building in my town. Do you know how many innocent people died in that blast?"

His insides twisted. *Six. Five office workers and a janitor, plus three injured ...*

Shaking himself out of it, he forced a shrug. "It's the job, but at the moment, so is keeping you alive." He pointed towards a plastic, office-style storage drawer cart. "If you get hungry, I've got some beef jerky and a couple of candy bars in one of the drawers over there." He turned away again, ready to leave, but the sound of metal scraping against the concrete floor sent him into alert. Instinctively he faced her, simultaneously fragmenting his body. She hoisted one of the smaller weights and threw it with all her might, right at his head. It passed through him and crashed into the door with a mighty thud. Her face fell.

"Also a nice try." He re-solidified so he could push the weight out of the way of the door. "Has DOSA improved their 'improvised weapons' training or are you just a scrapper?"

"Go to Hell."

"Already been there for a while, princess." He slipped out the door before locking it behind him. This couldn't have happened at a worse time. If one thing went wrong, it could all be over.

This job has always been about compromise. Is letting one woman die to get things done really unacceptable? Yeah, in this case, for me... it is.

He'd crossed so many lines, made so many hard choices to keep his position with the gang. This was one stand he had to take if he wanted to live with himself, though. Whatever it took, he couldn't let her die.

Chapter Three

Juliet glared at the door for a good minute after Sandstorm had disappeared through it. Maybe knocking the guy out—especially with his powers—and making a break for it had been a long shot, but dang, for a second there, she'd gotten her hopes up.

Okay, Juliet, so you screwed up, and you're in a bad position, but you're a freakin' Park. Parks don't give up. We're superheroes for a reason. What would Dad do?

Her heart sank. Dave Park probably wouldn't have jumped through a portal after a supervillain or rushed into a dangerous situation without backup. He planned ahead and took precautions—which was why he'd had his own DOSA team by the time he was thirty and Juliet was four years into her career with no hope of promotion due to a recent performance evaluation praising her for passion and quick thinking but reaming her for "repeated instances of recklessness during missions."

The thought of her father stirred regret within her. Had DOSA informed him about her disappearance yet? Did Shawn and their sister Abigail know? Mom? They'd all be so worried and it was her fault for being stupid. Bad things happening to her because she'd been an idiot was one thing. Causing her family grief was another.

She couldn't hurt them by not coming home.

Determination strengthened, she bent down to examine the disruptor cuff on her ankle. She knew from experience that the dang things were pretty much indestructible, but those were the DOSA versions. Maybe villains bought cheap knockoffs?

The cuff clamped around her showed no seams and had overlapping metal pieces that allowed it to expand

and contract to conform to any size or shape. She pried at it with her fingertips. No good.

She'd just have to work without her superpowers—until she could find a controller, at least. Getting out of the room would have to be her first goal.

Examining the door proved it to be heavy with no access to the lock on her side, so picking the lock was out. With her powers, she probably could've power-blasted it off its hinges, but no point in fussing about what she couldn't do.

K, so powers off the table. Lock picking off the table ... other exits? Air vents? Walls I can tunnel through?

Juliet circled the room, tracing the walls. The building appeared to be a mix of concrete and cinder block, and while she found a few vents, they were too small to get herself into. She let out a breath. Well, she'd already tried using Sandstorm's weights as a weapon. If he'd left those in the room, maybe there was something else.

She meticulously went over the room's contents. He'd left a tube of toothpaste, a bar of soap, and other toiletries in the bathroom, which consisted of a toilet, sink, and shower. At least she'd be able to do some basic grooming, though she hoped she wouldn't be staying there long enough that it would become an issue.

Returning to the main area, she examined the bed. It had a homemade appearance, crafted out of pallets with a mattress sitting on top of it. She pulled up the mattress but found nothing under it besides dust.

Finally there was the drawer cart. Drawer one contained the promised beef jerky and candy bars. Drawer two had a collection of ... comic books? She pulled the stack out of the drawer and thumbed through them out of curiosity. Apparently Sandstorm was into science fiction. She didn't even know *Firefly* had comic spin-offs.

Finding the drawer otherwise empty, she replaced the

books before opening the final drawer. A black case rested within. She pried this open and discovered a set of basic tools: a screwdriver, hammer, pliers, and tape measure. She picked up the hammer and considered its weight. Maybe she could use it as a weapon if pressed, but going at supervillains with a basic hammer probably wouldn't end well. Still, it was an option. This other stuff, though, wasn't much use unless she wanted to build a cabinet... wait a second!

An idea struck her, and she hurried back to the door. Yeah, the lock was on the outside, but the hinges were on the inside.

Picking up the screwdriver, she tossed it playfully into the air before catching it again. She listened for a long moment. Some sort of machinery, she thought maybe an air circulation system, droned in the distance, but other than that things were silent.

This was her chance to make it right. She unscrewed the bottom hinge first before making her way up the door. It started to lean but she caught it and eased it to the floor best she could. It still thudded far too loudly for her taste, the sound echoing down the empty corridor. She froze, listening for any sign of approaching supervillains.

Nothing.

Okay, she was out of her cell. Now what?

She glanced down at the disrupter cuff. Getting the cuff off would drastically improve her chances. She had no idea where this facility was located or how far she'd have to travel to get help. If it was in the middle of nowhere, she wouldn't want to have to trek out in her socks. They'd probably catch her. She didn't have an exact idea of all their powers, but flying was a rare enough ability that if she could get outside and take to the air, she couldn't imagine they'd be able to come after her.

The hallway she stood in dead-ended several doors down and all the doors leading off it appeared to be the same interior style as the one she'd just escaped from. That and the lack of windows made her suspect she was on a basement level. Going up might be her only way out. There was the elevator, but that was an enclosed space and if someone on the upper floor noticed it being summoned, they'd probably figure out it was her. Better to look for stairs.

Sticking the screwdriver into the hip pocket of her leggings in case she needed it later, she began trying doors. Several were locked, but the one at the very end, right next to the elevator, opened up into a small room, barely a closet, with a ladder ascending the wall towards a ship-style hatch. She peered up the ladder. Above, more fluorescent lights flickered, but she couldn't hear any voices or movement.

Well, I can't exactly stay here.

Senses on alert, she climbed, pausing every few rungs to listen for her captors. She reached the floor above. The ladder continued upward at least one more level. Should she risk poking around here for an exit or see what was up there first?

The space the ladder had let her out on was another small, closet-like room so she put her ear to the door and listened before making her move. All quiet. She opened the door and peeped out. Her lips pursed. This hallway looked identical to the one she'd just left, no sign of an exit. Maybe the next level was a better option.

She climbed again but this time found herself in an open space that resembled a large attic or the top of an aircraft hangar. Fans circled overhead, probably part of the air circulation system she'd heard from below. A metal catwalk went down the center with thin panels with light shining through them on either side in place of a more solid-looking floor. She was about to go back down and retry the previous level when murmured voices caught her attention. Sliding forward along the catwalk, she came to the second set of panels. In the center of this one was an air vent, and through it, she could see a room filled with computers.

Mentallica sat at one of the stations with someone pacing nearby, just out of view.

Juliet chewed her bottom lip. Maybe if she could get access to those computers she could contact someone in DOSA, but Mentallica and at least one other person were in her way.

"Why does Wallace always listen to that jackass?" an angry male voice grumbled, muffled, but still intelligible.

Hoping to hear something useful, Juliet lay on the ground and scooted out to look through the vent. Diamondback stopped pacing to hover over Mentallica who now wore a pair of blue-light glasses as she worked on the computer.

"Sandstorm has a proven record, plus you know he's a Lucas. That carries weight in this gang," she said.

"I don't care who the guy's family was, he's still making this take too long." Diamondback leaned against her desk, forcing himself into her field of view.

She pushed her computer chair back a foot or so. "I sense I'm not going to get any work done until you've finished whining so go ahead and get it out."

"It's not whining. It's fact. The guy makes us do everything the hard way. All the triple checking and pussyfooting around instead of going for the jugular. We've got so much firepower. Why aren't we using it?"

"His triple checking is the reason our cell has managed to stay active while every other team has been taken down by DOSA or fallen apart from within." Mentallica eyed him over her glasses. "Wallace knows that. I know that. I'm not really surprised you haven't gotten it through to your puny brain yet, though I *am* kind of shocked you know the word 'pussyfooting'."

"Whatever," he said. "Aren't you at all suspicious about this DOSA agent he won't let us kill? If he's all about the plan, why introduce a risk like her?"

"Because he's right—again," Mentallica said. "I don't like it either, but having a DOSA agent in our pocket could potentially pay off big time. Even if we only get a little intel out of it."

Juliet swallowed. Was that why they were keeping her alive? To interrogate her? That wouldn't last long. Even if she was the sort to betray her agency—which she wasn't— she wasn't high enough in DOSA to know anything useful to them. Not really. Once they figured that out, they'd dispose of her.

I need to find the way out of here—and fast.

"We wouldn't need intel if we just got the mission over with," Diamondback continued. "That's what's driving me nuts. We have the explosives in place, and the city's already primed for it with the last blast. What's stopping us from moving up the timeline? The longer the wait, the more chance DOSA will find them—"

"The payment method needs to be tested more," Mentallica said.

"Yeah, and it should've been done weeks ago." Disdain crept into Diamondback's tone. "It's your only job on this mission. What's taking so long?"

"I'm sorry, Huxley, I guess I'm not pulling my weight like you. You had the complicated job of planting a few explosive devices around the city using stolen teleportation technology you don't even understand." Her tone became exaggeratedly apologetic. "I don't know how I could be so silly as to think that my work creating a financial transfer system that will allow us to drain accounts in seconds with the funds being completely untraceable is as difficult as what you do. Of course, I'm also hacking into the emergency alert system to blast a QR code that victims can scan to give us said information and also which can't be overridden by authorities trying to stop us from accepting extortion payments from their citizenry. That's not important, though. It's such easy work compared to—"

"All right, all right!" Diamondback scowled. "I get it. You're a genius. No need to go on about it."

Mentallica crossed her arms over her chest, her expression smug.

Explosives, extortion ... QR codes? Juliet bit her bottom lip trying to figure this out. It clicked together. They were planning to use the explosive to blackmail the entire city! DOSA wouldn't bend to supervillain demands, but a panicked citizenry, aware that multiple bombs were planted around their city but with no idea where, totally would. Random individuals from all walks of life might be convinced to give away every cent they owned if the alternative was seeing schools, workplaces, and transportation hubs demolished. Even if it only managed to convince a percentage of those threatened, the Black Foxes could make off with millions of dollars in moments, all without lifting a finger or demolishing a single building.

What did Wallace say? They have five devices planted—four now that we got the one in that apartment building. They could be anywhere.

"We're running out of time, though. If the DOSA chick is right, they've already got one," Diamondback said. "They'll be looking for more—"

"If they start finding them, we'll move up the plan," a woman's voice said. Wallace entered the room, and Diamondback immediately snapped to attention. "It won't be ideal—I want every t crossed and i dotted—but we've invested far too much into this mission for it to fail. If it looks like DOSA is onto us, we'll pull a Hail Mary. Start the countdown and blast the QR code everywhere we can. Worst case scenario, DOSA's white-hats block our payment transfers, so we set off the bombs to retaliate." A cruel smile spread across the older woman's lips. "The good news is if we do that, we won't even have to plant bombs in the next city. With that much destruction on record, if we say we have devices ready to blow, they'll believe us and we can play the game again."

Juliet shuddered. She needed to find out where those bombs were before she escaped. Sandstorm had said something about remotely monitoring them, so there had to be information on their location and status. If she could just—

Someone grabbed her ankles and yanked her away from the vent.

Juliet gasped as she slid onto the catwalk. She twisted and turned, bracing her hands against the floor to bring herself into a seated position.

"You shouldn't be here," Sandstorm said.

Teeth gritting, she pushed through a kip-up, landing on her feet with her fist swinging towards his solar plexus. Her blows cut through him like he wasn't even there, only a tingling energy confirming that she'd made contact at all. All her momentum in the blows, she stumbled through him only to have him catch her by the arm, apparently solid again.

"Yeah, that's not going to work," he said. "Nice one with the door hinges though. I didn't see that—"

She slammed her fist down into the wrist of the hand holding her only to have him fragment again. With his body no longer solid, she wrenched away then dodged back, her fists in front of her.

"You do realize you can't hit me, right?" He arched an eyebrow.

What she wouldn't do to be able to throw a power blast right now. Her mind turned to the screwdriver in her pocket. Him being "unsolid" might mean she couldn't hit him, but it also meant he couldn't restrain her. If she tempted him into getting another hold on her, she might be able to strike fast before he got a chance to fragment.

"What's going on up there?" Wallace's voice barked from below. "Sandstorm, is that you?"

"I've got it under control," he shouted back, his eyes not leaving Juliet.

Juliet drew a deep breath. She'd only get one chance at this. Pulse pounding, she charged, barreling through his once again fragmented form off the catwalk. She spun around as he dove for her, grappling her arms to her sides, but her hand was already around the tool in her pocket.

"No, you don't." He pulled her against his chest. She drew the screwdriver and jabbed, aiming for his side. The weapon again whiffed through him as if he were made of air. This time, though, his hold on her arms remained solid. The tingling spread into her, sparking against her nerves like static electricity, before the floor beneath her gave like vapor and they both plummeted through it to the level below. She landed with a muffled shriek. He solidified on top of her, prying the screwdriver from her grasp.

"Let me go!" She squirmed.

"Hold still. I'm trying to—"

A door opened, and Sandstorm jumped up, pulling her to her feet as well, his fingers digging into her wrists.

Wallace and Diamondback stood in the doorway to the room they'd fallen into. Wallace's stern face did not look amused, though Diamondback had a smug smile.

"What's she doing out of her cell?" Wallace demanded.

Sandstorm held up the screwdriver before tossing it at Wallace's feet. "We must've missed this when we searched her. God only knows where she had it."

Diamondback eyed the tool as if it were radioactive, and Wallace didn't move to pick it up.

Juliet eyed Sandstorm. Did he not want to admit to not clearing her room well or did he not recognize the tool as his own? Either way, should she say something? Maybe get them fighting among themselves?

"Can you secure her or do we need to end this?" Wallace asked, her tone frigid.

"I've got it." Sandstorm pulled Juliet closer. She

elbowed him in the side and this time it hit. He wheezed but didn't release her.

"I told you this plan is stupid." Diamondback sneered. "We should just—"

"Things are already in motion," Sandstorm interrupted. "It's less risky to keep going than to reroute. We need to secure her better is all."

"Last chance," Wallace said. "If I find her outside of her cell again, we do it Diamondback's way."

Diamondback's grin widened, and Juliet's blood ran cold.

"That won't be necessary." Sandstorm eyed her. "It won't happen again." His voice took on a tone that weirdly reminded her of her dad. Man, she'd give anything to be scolded by her father for her idiocy right now.

"You should let me take care of her now, boss," Diamondback muttered.

"No one's taking care of anybody," Sandstorm said.

"Who's gonna stop me?" Diamondback moved forward, chest out, gaze burning into Sandstorm.

Juliet took a subtle step back. If they killed each other, it would increase her own chances of survival—well, maybe not if Diamondback were the survivor.

"Do you really want to do this?" Sandstorm said, his tone leveling to sound almost bored.

"You don't have it in you to take me down, Lucas," Diamondback hissed, his lips curling back to reveal his fangs. "You hide behind your plans and your precautions, but you're not man enough to—"

Sandstorm grabbed Diamondback by the shoulders and pushed down. The floor wavered and wobbled and sucked up the villain like quicksand until he was gone up to his waist. Diamondback lunged forward, jaws open, towards Sandstorm's arm. Sandstorm released him and jumped back, the floor solidifying once more with Diamondback still stuck in it. Diamondback shrieked and flailed, hammering his fists against the metal floor that was cinched around his midsection.

"I'm not man enough to what?" Sandstorm crossed his arms over his chest, looking down at his rival.

"Let me go!" Diamondback screamed. "I can't ... I can't breathe."

"Sounds like a personal problem," Sandstorm deadpanned.

"Lucas," Wallace said, her voice taking on an edge of warning. "You proved your point. Let him go."

Sandstorm's smile faded only to return accompanied by a mischievous glint in his eye. He bent down and held his hands against the floor. It rippled. With a shout, Diamondback dropped right through it, presumably to the floor below.

Wallace sighed. "Not what I meant, but I suppose I should've been more specific. Get her secure again, and remember, this mission is more important than your infighting with Huxley."

"Yes, ma'am." Sandstorm nodded to Juliet. "You want to walk or am I carrying you?"

"I'll walk." Juliet glared at him.

He escorted her to the elevator again. When the doors opened to the next level, Juliet feared Diamondback would be waiting, but apparently he'd decided to go pout somewhere. To her chagrin, Sandstorm pulled a pair of zip ties from his pocket and forced her hands together to bind her wrists.

"Sorry. Just until I've re-secured your room," he said.

"Whatever." She avoided his eyes, feeling pathetic. She sulked on the bed as he searched the room, gathering up various items that might prove useful in an escape attempt or as weapons. He then re-hung the door.

"You hungry?" he asked.

She angled away from him.

He came to stand before her. "Let me see your hands."

Juliet hesitated then held them up to him. He drew a multi-tool from his back pocket and cut through the zip ties.

"It's not personal," he then said. "You're safe for now. Don't try anything else stupid, and you might get through this." He turned and left, the door locking behind him again.

Juliet's chest tightened. Her first escape might not have gone as planned, but she'd get another chance. She had to.

Chapter Four

Shawn stroked his four-year-old daughter's soft, dark hair and smiled. She squeezed the stuffed Totoro toy that never left her side, burying her precious face into it. Shawn pulled the blankets around her then glanced at his wife who was settling their younger girl into her crib.

"Thank God, they're finally asleep," Katie breathed as Hana stretched out on her mattress.

Shawn put his finger to his lips before leading Katie out into the hall and shutting the door behind them. As soon as they were alone, he wrapped his arms around her and pulled her against his chest.

"You feeling okay?" he murmured.

"Better now." She hid her face in his T-shirt. "This morning was—rough."

He rubbed her upper back. "Do you want me to try and get tomorrow off? I've got some personal days saved up."

"No, save them for paternity leave. I'll need you more after this one gets here."

"Okay, but how about a cup of herbal tea and your choice of movie?" He traced his finger down her freckled nose before brushing a stray lock of red hair away from her face.

"You're my hero." She turned her face up for a kiss.

He pressed his lips against hers. One hand strayed to her waist, resting lightly over her midsection. The thought of another baby—half him, half her—stirred something within him, and he drew her closer, deepening his kiss.

"Or, you know, we could do other activities." He moved his mouth onto her neck.

"Activities?" She hummed.

"I think the kids call it 'Netflix and chill' these days," he teased.

"The kids, huh? You're not that hip, Shawn."

"I can be hip." He nibbled on her earlobe. She giggled.

His phone went off in his back pocket.

He released her. "Hold that thought."

She slipped away from him. "I'll go pick out a movie. I'm not forgetting you owe me tea."

Shawn checked his phone, considering sending it to voicemail. The display read simply, "Dad."

He'd just seen his father a few hours before when he was clocking out from DOSA HQ. Dave Park hadn't said anything about calling later. Hopefully it wasn't a work emergency.

He answered while starting down the hall to the kitchen. "Hey, Dad. What's up?"

"You ... are you ... something happened."

Shawn froze at the kitchen door. He didn't like his father's tone right now. "What do you mean?"

"I just got off the phone with Pangolin from the Pittsburgh branch," his father continued.

Shawn's heart stopped. Jules was stationed in Pittsburgh—

"Is Jules okay?" he stammered.

Katie poked her head out of the living room and looked at him quizzically.

"We're not ... it's not good, but it's also not ... they're not sure." His father sounded defeated. "Apparently she rushed into an encounter with a Black Fox. Her team lost contact, but they had them surrounded. No way out, or so they thought—but when they cleared the room she wasn't there and neither was the villain."

Shawn braced himself with one hand against the wall. Dang it, Jules. "Why'd she go in without backup?"

"I don't know ... well, I sort of do." Irritation flavored Dave's words. "You know your sister."

"Yeah—" Shawn drew the word out, massaging his forehead. "They ... do they know anything yet?"

"No. This ... I'm not going to lie, Shawn. This is bad. I'm ... not sure what I'm going to tell your mother."

Shawn slid down the wall to sit in the hallway, his insides twisting and untwisting. He'd just talked to her. She'd been in a good mood, laughing—taking stupid risks sure, but not like this.

I should've said something. I should've told her to be careful, to be smart, but would she have listened? No, she never listens. Dang you, Juliet. You're going to break Mom's heart ... you're going to break mine.

No. He couldn't accept this. He was not going to lose his baby sister to supervillains. Not like this.

"I've got this, Dad." He pulled himself off the floor. Katie came over and touched his upper arm, her eyes filled with worry. "I'll get the first flight out."

"What's your plan?" He could hear his father's frown.

"Plan? I'm not sure, but someone needs to be there to make sure DOSA is looking out for her instead of covering their butts." Shawn had had his own experiences with DOSA's lack of loyalty to its heroes. Whatever her mistakes, he was not going to let them cut her off from help to save face and keep to protocol.

"I was planning on doing that, but I might be of more use going over the Pittsburgh team leader's head, calling in some favors up the chain." There was a long pause.

Shawn felt something brush his hand and looked down to see Katie's fingers wrap around his. He forced a smile before turning his attention back to the phone call.

"You think you can handle the Pittsburgh team?" Dave asked.

"I learned from the best," Shawn said, trying to sound confident.

"All right. You've got this. Thanks, Shawn. Oh ... what about Katie and the girls? Do you want your mother over there? Would Katie want that?"

Shawn made eye contact with his wife. "I'm not sure. I'll ask her and text you later, okay?"

"Of course. Whatever you need. I hate to draw you away from her right now. It's just—" Dave paused. "When you told me this morning, I was over the moon, you know? Like I was the happiest man in the world. Now ... I feel like everything is crashing down. Even something as amazing as a new grandbaby—we have to get her back, Shawn. We have to."

"We will." Shawn kept his voice firm. "We will, Dad. I promise."

"All right. Talk to Katie and keep me posted. I love you, son."

"I love you too." Shawn hung up the phone and faced Katie. "Did you hear any of that?"

"Something happened to Juliet?" She tightened her hold on his hand. "And you're going to Pittsburgh to help?"

"That's the short version—though admittedly, I don't know a lot of details of the long yet." He touched her cheek. "Will you be okay alone for a few days right now? I can have my mother come over. She'd love to take the girls off your hands."

"I might take her up on that, but I know her number. If I get overwhelmed, I'll call." She stood on her tiptoes to kiss his cheek. "Right now, you need to focus on getting your sister home safely, all right? You're a hero, Shawn. Go do what you're good at."

Chapter Five

Juliet sat on the edge of the pallet bed, staring into space. She had thought about taking a shower, but the idea of getting naked in enemy territory didn't appeal to her. Plus the only clothes she had were the ones she was wearing, already grimy and soaked with fear sweat.

Time was hard to mark without natural light or a timepiece of any kind. She'd searched the room again, but Sandstorm's second attempt at clearing it had been far more thorough. The best she got were a couple of loose nails. Desperate, she tucked these under her mattress, just in case.

Her stomach grumbled. Sandstorm hadn't cleared out the jerky and candy bars, thankfully, so she devoured those, washed down with tap water from the bathroom sink.

Running out of ways to stay active, she picked up one of the comic books Sandstorm had left behind and thumbed through it. This one was *Star Wars*. Weird choice of entertainment for a grown man, especially a supervillain. Not that she could throw stones. She still watched cartoons whenever she took a lazy day off and had once cosplayed as Katara from *Avatar: The Last Airbender* when she had gone to a convention with some friends.

The sound of the bolt lock interrupted her reading. She tensed and set the comic book aside.

The door opened, and Mentallica entered carrying a paper plate with a single sandwich on it. Behind her, Sandstorm loomed, his tall frame blocking the exit, probably so Juliet didn't make a break for it. This time he wasn't wearing his leather jacket, instead only a form-fitting, plain gray T-shirt. Super form-fitting. Like she didn't know if she could get a finger between the cuff of his sleeve and his bicep. Plus his pecs—her face burned and she forced herself to look away.

Dang, is he intentionally buying his shirts two sizes too small?

"Nah, though yeah, I get it," Mentallica suddenly said. "He's had the same wardrobe since he joined my team over two years ago, but that was before he took up lifting. I admire the gains, but he really needs to upgrade his T-shirt collection. Maybe he likes being eye candy, though."

"Huh?" Sandstorm and Juliet said simultaneously.

"DOSA-Girl's getting a little pheromone-induced Stockholm Syndrome," Mentallica said.

"I am not!" Juliet snarled.

"Mind reader." Mentallica tapped her forehead. "Can't hide from me."

"Whatever." Juliet stood and snatched the plate from Mentallica's hand. "Doesn't matter. I'm only into guys with souls. Not supervillains." She stared pointedly at Sandstorm's face, very intentionally avoiding anything from his neck down. His hazel eyes widened in bemusement before his expression turned grave and he glanced over his shoulder.

"I haven't seen Diamondback in a while. Have you?"

"Probably in his room sulking." Mentallica pulled a wad of brown, fast-food-chain-style napkins out of her pocket and offered them to Juliet. She took them. Thankfully they appeared to be unused, just crumpled. Mentallica then turned away and exited the room, still talking to Sandstorm. "Wallace told me about you putting him in the floor. Did you have to antagonize the dude—"

The door shut behind them, cutting off Juliet's ability to listen in. She picked at the sandwich. A couple of slices of thin lunch meat and mayo and mustard between two pieces of basic white bread. If she stayed here too long, she'd get scurvy. Well, food was food. Good to keep her strength up.

After eating, she paced for a while before returning to the comic books. She'd just finished the second one when the lights around her dimmed. Some sort of day-night lighting they used to approximate natural light maybe? She kind of suspected this place was underground. Fitting for a villain lair but irritating to escape. There still had to be an exit and entrance, though. They weren't teleporting in and out every time—were they?

Her eyes stung, but trying to bed down here would be like sleeping knowing there was a spider in the room. Her skin crawled at the thought.

If I don't get rest, though, I won't be sharp, and I might miss a chance to escape.

Trying to maintain some semblance of normalcy, she went into the bathroom and found the toothpaste. There was a cabinet under the sink that had a bottle of men's body wash in it. Handy if she decided to use the shower later. She opened it and gave it a sniff.

Hmm. Smells ... tree-y. Why do dudes get all the cool scents?

Continuing her investigation, she found an electric razor, a first aid kit that included a lot of snake-bite bandages, and a stick of deodorant. Apparently he'd left most of his toiletries behind, but maybe he had backups stashed somewhere ... or he didn't plan for her to be in his room for long. There was also an unopened package with a couple of toothbrushes in it, so she went ahead and took one to brush her teeth before washing her face.

Hygiene seen to, she crossed the room to turn off the main light but left the light in the bathroom on so she wouldn't be completely in the dark if something happened. She slipped off her socks—taking a moment to rub her ankle around the disruptor cuff—but kept the remainder of her clothing. She then slipped under the thin blankets. Could be worse. She buried her face in the pillow—dang, it smelled like that body wash. Weird.

She rolled onto her back so her nose wouldn't be right up against the pillowcase and stared at the shadows on the ceiling. She'd made so many mistakes today, but tomorrow? Tomorrow she'd do something to fix them.

The muffled sound of footfalls caused her to angle towards the door again. They paused immediately outside. Then, like mist slipping through cracks, a weird haze seeped around the door. It didn't look gaseous, though, more like a cloud of tiny particles, moving as one like a flock of starlings in a murmuration. The swarm moved upward, solidifying first into a pillar and then into the shadowy outline of a tall man carrying something.

She jumped out of bed, her arms springing into a guard stance.

"Easy." The voice was Sandstorm's. He shook the object in his hand and it unfolded into a ... lawn chair?

"What's that for?" She frowned.

"To sit in," he said simply.

She groaned. "Well, that's one mystery solved. What do you want?"

"Nothing." He set the chair near the door, angled so he could see both the door and her without turning his head, before sitting down.

Juliet swallowed. "Did you want to talk or something?"

"Nope." He leaned back, fiddling with something in his hand. Whatever it was, it was small—too small to be a weapon she thought—and it glinted in the low light seeping out of the bathroom. Maybe a coin.

"Try and get some sleep," he said. "I'll be quiet."

"Uh, how about no?" She sat on the edge of the bed, staring daggers at him. In the dim light, she couldn't see his face. Maybe she should turn the lights back on.

"I'm not going to try anything, I promise." He held up his hands. "Just sitting."

"Yeah, but you're a supervillain and holding me hostage so your trust points are pretty much a negative balance, Sandy."

"Suit yourself." He rested one foot on the opposite knee and turned his attention back to the door.

Dang it. Was he really going to keep sitting there? For how long? How did he expect her to sleep with him lurking like that? Fat chance.

She continued to sit, staring at him staring at the door. Minutes ticked by—at least she thought they did. If only she had a watch or something. Her eyes watered and her vision swam. Was he serious? She wanted to sleep!

"You do realize how creepy this is, right, dude?"

"Sorry."

"So ..." She nodded towards the door.

"I want to be sure you're safe is all," he said.

"I'd feel a lot safer if I were alone," she shot back.

"Maybe you'd feel that way, but you wouldn't be. Trust me." Even in the dark, she could hear the wry smile in his tone.

Sensing he wasn't giving up, she scooted so she could rest her back against the wall. "Is your secondary superpower being irritating?"

"Nah, that's just years of practice."

"Whatever." She moved her pillows and blankets around so she could sit comfortably and waited.

Maybe if she didn't engage with him, he'd get bored— or fall asleep so she could tie his shoelaces together or something. That was a thought. If she outlasted him, maybe she could overpower him. Of course, with the door locked from the outside and him having come in with his powers, even if she did manage to knock him out or tie him up, she'd still be stuck in the room. Though if he had a disruptor remote on him, she might be able to get her powers back. One good power blast could probably take down the door. She simply needed to wait until he was out.

They sat in silence, a weird mix of anxiety and absolute boredom churning within her. After he continued to stay still and quiet, though, not even really looking at her, she relaxed a little. If he wanted to attack her, he would've done it already. He was strong enough that even without taking his powers into account, he probably didn't need to wait for her guard to be down to hurt her.

Her head nodded forward. Sleep sounded so good right now—

Something thudded in the hallway. Juliet jerked upright, heart in her throat. Sandstorm leaned forward in his chair, his posture taut.

"What—"

He put his finger to his lips and rose from his chair. There came another thump, followed by a muttered string of profanity. Was that Diamondback?

The deadbolt screeched as someone undid the lock. The door opened, and Diamondback stumbled in.

"Hey, little hero," he slurred.

Sandstorm sprang forward, grappled him, and pulled him right through the wall.

Juliet jumped to her feet, heart pounding. Banging and shouting echoed from where the men had disappeared then all went quiet. The wall rippled, and Sandstorm stepped back through, adjusting his jacket.

"What did you do to him?" Juliet stammered.

"Shoved him in the storage closet. He's not getting out of there, even if he wasn't too drunk to see straight." He dusted his hands off on his jeans and folded up the lawn chair. "You should be safe until morning at which point I'll let Wallace know what he was up to and she'll put him back in line."

Cold washed through her. "You knew he was going to try something?"

"Knew? Not really. Educated guess? Sure." He pushed the door shut behind him and crossed the room to stand where the light from the bathroom fell across his face. His eyes glistened in the dim glow. "I knew he was angry at you being here, at me for showing him up earlier in front of Wallace, and ... well, I knew he was drinking, and he's a mean drunk. If I didn't have my powers, he'd have taken my head off the last time he got smashed."

"He's not great even when he's sober from what I can see, so I believe it." She rubbed her arms. With the crisis over, a chill overcame her.

"Get some sleep. Like I said, you should be safe until morning." His body shimmered as he accessed his powers again.

"Thank you!" she said quickly.

He paused, looking at her. "No problem." Breaking into particles again, he swept under the door.

Juliet pulled the blankets around herself once more. What was going on with this guy?

Chapter Six

Sandstorm's legs dangled off the end of the break room sofa. His leather jacket, which he'd laid over himself as a makeshift blanket, didn't do much against the constantly circulating air from the ventilation system. He shuddered and opened his eyes.

I need to check on the Park girl.

He stood and stretched quickly before shouldering his jacket and exiting the room into the hall. His pace quickened as he drew near her door. A repeated thudding and crashing echoed down the corridor. Was it coming from her room? No. Seemed like the next door down.

Diamondback.

He let out a breath. If Diamondback were still contained, Juliet Park was safe. Unfortunately, he couldn't keep that jackass in there forever.

Stopping in front of the door he called out, "You gonna behave yourself if I let you out of there?"

The banging stopped. Sandstorm flooded his powers into the padlock holding the closet shut so he could remove it without a key then opened the door.

Diamondback burst out, fists swinging, only to crash through Sandstorm's faded body, swerve violently to the side, and topple into the door frame. His eyes were bloodshot and he smelled like pee.

Sandstorm stumbled back a step, pinching his nose. "Dude. How wasted were you last night?"

Diamondback swayed for a moment before sneering at Sandstorm. "I'm going to kill you someday."

"Great team-building exercise, murder," Sandstorm said dryly. "I think I've already proven that I've got an edge over you in a fight, but even if I didn't, we're on the same team, working towards the same goal. You being an idiot is going to get us all killed. I'm not against you. I'm just not going to let you do something stupid."

"Sure. You're in it for the 'team.'" Diamondback laughed bitterly. "You may have the boss and Mentallica fooled, but you're looking out for your own sneaky self, not the team. I don't know how I'll prove it, but I will." His whole face contorted in rage. "What if I told Wallace you spent last night in the prisoner's room?"

"Do you really want to face Wallace right now?" Sandstorm arched his eyebrows. "Hungover and smelling like the floor of a dive bar's bathroom? You know she doesn't like you drinking during critical mission stages."

"Because of you we've been at a critical mission stage for months!" Diamondback's rank breath caused Sandstorm to instinctively fragment. It didn't help. "I haven't had a chance to cut loose in ages, and you won't even let me have a little fun messing with our hostage!"

Sandstorm's resolve strengthened. "You try to 'mess' with her again, and I'll meld you into a wall instead of just pushing you through one."

"Yeah, I get it. Special Sandflake wants to keep all the fun for himself."

Sandstorm rolled his eyes. "Sandflake? Really? Are you sure you aren't still drunk? Go take a shower, Huxley. With how you smell, we're lucky DOSA hasn't found the lair just by following their noses."

Diamondback dodged forward to grab his arm, but his fingers sank right through Sandstorm.

"Everything okay down there?" Mentallica's voice called from the other end of the hallway.

"Yeah, Diamondback was just leaving." Still fragmented to avoid any attacks, Sandstorm turned his back on Diamondback who swore under his breath before stomping away—hopefully to take that shower. Man, the guy smelled.

"What's up with you two?" Mentallica crossed her

arms over her chest. She was wearing an olive green hoodie and had a small backpack on.

"He got drunk last night and tried to pay our hostage a 'visit,'" Sandstorm explained. "I stopped him, and he's pissed."

Mentallica glanced around Sandstorm at Diamondback's retreating form. "Creep. Do you think he'll try again? We're supposed to deal with Surge, and if we're both gone it'll be him and Wallace alone."

Sandstorm hesitated. Wallace was cold-blooded, probably didn't give a damn if Juliet lived or died, but she'd agreed to the plan. If they tried to compromise Surge and it turned out Juliet wasn't around to provide proof of life—or had been abused to the point where Surge lost it and started blasting—they'd lose the asset.

"I'll tell Wallace to keep an eye on him. When we get back, though, do you think you can find where he's stashing the booze? He's not supposed to have access to that right now, and he's dumb when he's drunk."

"You mean 'dumber,' right?" Mentallica sniffed. "I'll see about it. If you want I can send Wallace the warning telepathically so we don't have to go find her."

"Yeah, smart. We're already running late."

She nodded and closed her eyes, concentrating on her powers to send the message, he assumed.

Sandstorm rubbed at his eyes. Even knowing that Diamondback had been dealt with, he hadn't slept much. This whole thing was getting far too complicated. Too many chainsaws to juggle, all of which would cut him to pieces if he lost focus for a moment. His hand strayed to his pocket to finger the metal disk.

I've got this. I'm not going to let up—just get through it—

"You playing with that thing again?" Mentallica asked.

Sandstorm yanked his hand out of his pocket. "Habit."

"Yeah ..." She eyed him skeptically. "You ever going to tell me the truth about why you carry an old bottle cap around?"

"Nope." He winked at her.

She shoved him. He kept his powers down, even rocking back dramatically at her push.

"Hey, watch it. I'm delicate."

"You're an idiot. Let's get going."

They took the elevator up to the staging room. Once there, Mentallica walked over to the vault where they kept the spare teleportation disks and entered the code.

"Don't forget to bring a spare," Sandstorm said. The last thing he wanted was to get stranded if their teleporter chose to burn out. Generally the things were good for about four jumps before they were toast, but the energy discharge could be unpredictable. Some could only manage a single leap.

"Already on it." She pocketed one disk and held the other out in front of her. "Where should we port in?"

"What's our closest anchor point to DOSA HQ? My intelligence says Surge made it into the city late last night, and that's the first place he'd go."

"We have one a few blocks from there." Mentallica turned the dial on the back of the disk.

While the disks were by far the best form of existing transportation, they had their limits. For one, they were expensive. For another, they could only open portals to where an anchor point had been left, a secondary disk, essentially, placed at a location that they intended to port to. The third problem, of course, was the huge expenditure of energy that caused power grid spikes that DOSA had learned to track—but that just meant they'd have to move fast.

Mentallica hit the button, and a glowing blue portal expanded before them. They stepped through into a shadowy alleyway between two larger buildings. As the portal shut behind them, Sandstorm took in his surroundings. No one around. Just the normal traffic sounds from outside the alley.

"Let's move."

Mentallica pulled the hood of her jacket up over her face before fishing in her backpack and withdrawing a ball cap and a pair of sunglasses. "You never remember to hide your face."

"Don't need to. You always bring extras." He put the hat and glasses on. Not a perfect disguise, but he knew how to avoid security cameras and it wasn't like his face was well-known. Getting this close to a DOSA office was dangerous, of course, but the idea was to fly under the radar and make contact with Surge without the other agents catching on.

They stopped across the street from the mundane-looking office building DOSA's local team used as an HQ.

"Any ideas for how we get him out to talk to him?" he asked.

"Got this." Mentallica withdrew a phone from her back pocket. Sandstorm blinked when he recognized the purple, galaxy-themed phone case.

"You sure that's safe to use?" he asked. "They're probably tracking it."

"Got it covered. I installed some of my own software on it. Should bounce the signal around so that even if they are doing a track right now, they'll assume she's on the other side of the city. Never doubt me." She pulled up the contacts. "The guy's name is what? I doubt he's in here as 'Surge.'"

"Shawn Park." Sandstorm drew them both down another alleyway. They sank into the shadows.

"Shawn-Bawn?" Mentallica asked. "That was the last person who called her."

"Probably." Sounded like a dumb sibling nickname. "Do they have the Burnr app? That should be encrypted even if DOSA's watching."

"Yeah, they do."

"Good. Send him a message via her account. Tell him he needs to come out and meet with us. Give him a location a little ways from here but warn him if he tells anyone, she'll get hurt." His discomfort intensified, but he muscled through it.

She tapped the phone for a moment then showed him the unsent message.

He nodded. "Looks good. Go ahead and send."

"The only thing I'm not sure of is if he'll take the risk to come out and talk with us on his own." Mentallica hit send. "It's kind of an idiot move. We could be an ambush for all he knows."

"If he thinks it'll give his sister a chance to survive?" Sandstorm frowned. "Yeah, he'll come. Trust me."

A little down the street, they entered another alleyway that dead-ended up against a concrete wall. Sandstorm took his teleportation disk out, just in case. If Surge did bring along backup, they'd port out immediately.

Mentallica closed her eyes. Sandstorm watched her, waiting for any word. She could scan the brains of people around them like she were browsing through a Twitter feed, not going in-depth with any particular thought pattern but catching enough of a glimpse to know if they were her target. After several minutes, she let out a low whistle.

"You're right. He's coming, and from what's on his mind, he's alone. I'll keep reading him, though."

Sandstorm slipped the disk into his pocket and watched the entrance to the alleyway.

After a long moment, a figure stepped into view. Dark circles shadowed the hero's eyes, and his hair and civilian clothes, a button-up shirt and slacks, were rumpled. From the way the shirt stretched, Sandstorm was fairly confident he wore his uniform beneath it. The guy's face pinched when he saw the two villains waiting in the shadows, but he didn't move towards them, instead, standing back, eyeing them like a cornered animal.

Guilt twisted at Sandstorm. *He's worried about his sister, and can you blame him?*

A familiar, itching sensation in the back of his mind, like the suspicion he was being watched but ten times worse, snapped his attention to Mentallica. He thought directly at her.

Keep your attention on the target, not me.

You're being weird again. Her voice echoed blandly in his head.

Believe it or not, this isn't going to be fun for me.

She snorted. *It was your idea. If you're having second thoughts, we can just return to the lair and take care of her the old fashioned way. I'm sure Diamondback will volunteer if you're still squeamish.*

Sandstorm set his mouth firm. *No. I've got this. Use your powers to get him here.*

A second later, Surge started, the usual response to having Mentallica suddenly talking in his head. He hopped off the ground, hovered for a moment, then glided down the alley towards them. Knowing Mentallica's powers wouldn't work right if he used his own, Sandstorm resisted the urge to draw her into his fade but kept himself fragmented with his hand close enough to her that he could grab her if Surge suddenly attacked.

"Where's my sister?" the hero asked through clenched teeth.

"Safe. For now," Sandstorm said simply. "Whether she remains so depends entirely on your willingness to cooperate."

"What do you mean?" Surge asked.

"It's pretty simple," Mentallica put in. "We're working an operation here. One that would be better off without DOSA interference. Your sister tried to interfere, but we dealt with her. That said, we don't have any reason to keep her around. We were hoping you, as a trusted member of DOSA's inner circle, might give us one."

Surge swallowed, his Adam's apple bobbing visibly. Sandstorm's hand brushed up against his pocket where the bottle cap rested, but he managed to keep his calm without reaching for it for once.

"I don't ... I'm not anything special. Not even a team leader. Just a regular DOSA hero," Surge said. "I don't know what you think I can offer you—"

"You're a Park," Sandstorm forced as much derision into his tone as he could muster. "A legacy sable. Even if you officially don't have the clout, your name alone opens doors. The question is, will you open them for us if it will save your sister?"

Surge's shoulders slumped. "I ... I don't have anything to give you... If it's money you want, I can put together a ransom. I'll need a little bit of time, but I swear—"

"You'd never be able to put together enough to interest us," Mentallica interrupted. "Unless you can scrape together a couple of million, which, based on the financial records you are now so desperately going over in your brain, I sense you cannot."

"I don't ... what do you want, then?" Surge asked.

Sandstorm squared his shoulders and took a step closer. "We want to know everything DOSA knows about our presence here. We want to know exactly what they are planning to do about it, and if anything changes, we want an update immediately."

Surge's lower lip went slack then his face hardened. "I won't do that. You're villains. You hurt people. I won't have blood on my hands."

"Just your sister's." Mentallica waved her phone. "I guess I'll text our boss and let her know we don't need the prisoner anymore. Hopefully she makes it quick. Want me to see if she can put it on video call for you?" She started to text.

"Stop!" Surge stammered.

Mentallica paused, gazing at him over the top of her phone.

"How do I know you'll keep your word?" Surge asked. "How do I know that she's even alive?"

Mentallica tapped on her phone for a moment. "I thought you might ask, so I took the liberty of installing a webcam where we're holding her." She turned the phone around, exhibiting Juliet Park sitting on the edge of her bed, chin in hand, staring blankly into space.

"That could be recorded," Surge said slowly. "Not actually proof of anything. Can I talk to her?"

"No, but I thought you might say that, so I included a 'ping' feature, so to speak. When I tap the screen, the camera will make a buzzing sound. Say when and see if she reacts."

Surge waited a moment before saying, "Now."

Mentallica tapped the screen. Juliet's head immediately jerked up, and her eyes darted around the room.

Surge shook his head. "You could fake that. It's not proof. I want to talk to her—"

"No, you don't," Mentallica interrupted. "Well, you do, but that's not what you're doing right now. Right now you're thinking if you can stall this, if you can keep us here a little longer, your DOSA friends will track you and take us in so you can force us to give your sweet baby sister back. You're thinking you need to buy time. Forget that."

Surge stiffened.

"If my colleague and I don't check in with our team, they'll assume this went sideways, and your sister won't be of any use to them," Sandstorm said. "My friend here is a mind reader, as I'm guessing you've deduced by now, as well as a grade-A hacker. If you tell anyone you're compromised, we'll know, and your sister will die. If you don't turn over the information we want, she dies."

"She's just a kid," Surge's voice cracked. "You ... please, you have to give me another way. I'll do ... almost anything."

"Someone once told me being a hero was about hard choices," Sandstorm continued. "Maybe the reason I never had the stomach for it, but you? You're all in on the hero game. I guess you need to decide if your hard choice is cooperating with us, or knowing that your sister died because you wouldn't play ball."

Surge closed his eyes then opened them again, glaring straight at Sandstorm with hatred Sandstorm knew he fully merited. He focused on his poker face, prompted partially by that itching feeling he always got when Mentallica was probing at him.

"What do you want me to do?" Surge asked.

"For now. Hold tight. We'll be in touch." Sandstorm nodded to Mentallica and then backed up a few steps, her following. Not wanting to risk Surge trying his sister's trick and hitching a ride back to the lair, he used his powers to step himself and Mentallica both through the wall at the end of the alley before activating his teleportation disk.

Safe inside the lair, he rolled his shoulders, trying to get his muscles to relax.

"Do you think he'll really go along with it?" Mentallica said.

"If he believed my bluff about us knowing if he tells anyone he's compromised? Yeah, I think we've got him," Sandstorm answered. "We do need to keep an eye on him, though. You think you can get access to his devices without DOSA knowing?"

"Yeah, but there's no way I can listen in on him constantly, and you know my powers won't reach that far," she said.

"I'm counting on him not wanting to take chances with his sister's life—"

"So it worked?" They both turned to see Wallace standing in the doorway.

"Yeah, he's in our pocket," Sandstorm said. "I suggest we use him carefully, though. DOSA keeps a close eye on their sables, and they've had enough issues with dirty agents in the past that they'll notice if we use him carelessly. He's a good asset. We need to be strategic."

"Good." She nodded slowly. "Diamondback told me about last night. His version of it anyway."

"Did his version involve him being sloppy drunk and stupid?" Sandstorm asked.

"No. He conveniently left that out. Just said you two got into a scuffle and you shoved him into a closet for the night. Oh, and that we shouldn't trust you."

"And you said?" Mentallica tilted her head to one side.

"I told him if he was bad enough at his job to lose to you in a fight, he needed to toughen up. I don't work with losers." A cold smile quirked Wallace's mouth before her eyes darkened again. "That said, the same goes for you, Lucas. If you and Diamondback kill each other, that means a larger share of the pot for me. If your little measuring contest puts the mission at risk, though. I'll kill both of you." She focused on Sandstorm, and a tightness gripped his throat, like invisible hands. He held his form solid, even though he could fragment out of her telekinetic grasp. If she was using her powers to threaten him, she was serious. He needed her to know he wouldn't flinch.

"I won't do anything stupid," he said. "You might want to convey the same message to Diamondback, though."

"I already did." Wallace turned away. "One of you needs to feed the prisoner. If we're keeping her around for a while, there's no point in starving her."

"Will do," Sandstorm said.

Mentallica gave a low whistle as soon as Wallace was gone. "She had you in a choke, didn't she? She must be serious if she's threatening you like that. You okay?"

"Meh. I'm not frightened by her sorcerer's ways."

Mentallica's brows furrowed. "Huh? Is that some kind

of *Dungeons and Dragons* reference?"

"Really?" he said. "You didn't get that—never mind. I'm going to go make sure the Park girl has something to eat."

"Sure, nerd boy." Mentallica walked off.

Sandstorm reached into his pocket, gripping his bottle cap until his fingers hurt.

Focus.

He'd bought Juliet Park a little more time. Hopefully it would be enough.

Chapter Seven

Juliet lay on her bed, staring at the ceiling and blowing through her pursed lips to make raspberry sounds.

She hadn't seen anyone that morning, and her stomach was grumbling. It had to be fairly late, way past when she'd usually eat breakfast—well—past when she'd usually chug a large coffee with three sugars and a good dash of cream to suppress her appetite until lunch in favor of pure caffeine ... but she was still hungry.

It had definitely been hours since Diamondback's thumping and banging on the walls had woken her up. At first, she'd been afraid he would somehow get out to go after her again, but instead he'd stopped, and she'd heard muffled arguing. He hadn't tried anything today, though she couldn't bring herself to feel safe. Every time she heard footsteps or a door opening or even when the ventilation system kicked on, she jumped.

Bored, hungry, and terrified. The worst trio in the history of ever.

A light tapping on the door caused her to sit up, inhaling sharply.

"Hey, it's me, Sandstorm. I've got some food for you. Can I come in?" he called out.

He was asking permission to enter? What kind of a supervillain was he?

"Yeah," she called out.

He didn't open the door, instead pouring himself through the cracks around it like a swarm of gnats. When he reformed as himself, he held a paper bowl with a plastic spoon sticking out. "It's oatmeal. Cinnamon apple flavored. I hope that's okay, 'cause it was that or plain. We're running low on supplies again."

"It's more than fine." She stood and accepted it from him. "What happened with Diamondback?"

"Nothing really." He shrugged. "Wallace gave us both a lecture about putting our beef before the mission, but it's not something he hasn't heard before. The guy doesn't like me much."

"Small dog syndrome." She sniffed. "My aunt had a chihuahua like that. Dang thing would nip at the ankles of everyone, including much bigger dogs. Four pounds of pure spite."

"Sounds like Diamondback." A faint smile crossed Sandstorm's face. "Though I don't know why you're throwing shade at anyone for being 'small,' short stuff. Do you weigh much more than that chihuahua?"

She wrinkled her nose at him. "Whatever, Sandy."

He laughed quietly and something stirred in her chest. She felt—safer somehow. Her eyes dropped to her oatmeal. This was stupid. Sure, he'd protected her last night, but he was still a villain. She was still his prisoner, maybe a valuable one, but a prisoner nonetheless.

I can't trust him. I can't trust any of them. Why does he have to pretend to be kind? It only makes it worse. What would've happened to me, though, if he hadn't interfered last night?

"I better get going. I'll be back later with something else for you to eat." He glanced her up and down. "I might ask Mentallica if she has some clothes you can borrow. It might not be a perfect fit, but you'll at least be able to change and take a shower."

"I'd appreciate that," she murmured.

He took a step away from her. Panic raced through her at the thought of being alone in this awful room again, so quiet, stuck with only her own thoughts and the threat that Diamondback might return.

"Wait!" she gasped.

Sandstorm looked at her quizzically.

"Do you think Diamondback will try anything again?"

she stammered. "Like ... like tonight?"

"I'd like to think he wouldn't be dumb enough, but honestly, I'm not sure." He grew thoughtful for a moment. "I know where there's a folding cot I can drag in here and put in front of the door. If it would make you feel better, I can sleep in here tonight."

"Yeah, it would," she said, and to her surprise she meant it.

He nodded slowly. "I'll see you then. For now, I'll just make sure I know what he's up to today. I'll see if Mentallica will keep tabs on him too. She's hard on creeps, as she calls them."

"Creeps is an apt description," she muttered.

Without another word, he slipped beneath the door again, leaving her to pick at her oatmeal.

What was she thinking? Begging for his help? Could she get any more pathetic?

But ...

He had protected her last night. He had treated her respectfully when it was likely no one would stop him from doing otherwise. Sandstorm might be a villain, but he didn't seem to be a monster like Diamondback.

Still, I can't let him get to me. I can't let myself trust him. Not really. That said ... maybe I could get him to trust me. Maybe if he thinks I'm a compliant, good little hostage, he'll get careless. Maybe getting closer to him is my ticket out of here. It's worth a shot. What do I have to lose after all?

Chapter Eight

Shawn sat in the empty break room of the HQ building, staring at the blank wall. A Styrofoam cup of now cold coffee rested before him.

What am I going to do?

The door behind him opened, and Pangolin entered. The Pittsburgh team leader was in his mid-thirties, balding, with a weathered face that made him look older than he was. Jules often referred to the square-jawed man as a "rock troll." The memory of this made Shawn almost smile only to have the dull ache of anxiety swell up in his stomach and push the mirth down.

"You holding on all right?" Pangolin asked.

"Not really," Shawn said.

"I'm sorry we haven't been able to find anything yet. We weren't prepared for this to happen." The wrinkles around Pangolin's eyes deepened. "I don't mean to victim-blame—"

"It's fine. I know my sister can be reckless." Shawn stood. "Honestly, I'm tired, and it's getting late. I need to find a hotel for the night. You'll call me if you find anything?"

"Of course, but there's no need to get a hotel." Pangolin opened the door. "We have spare quarters for visiting sables. I had Klaxon prep room 304 for you. She even scraped up some basic toiletries. I think she steals them from hotels when we travel, but don't tell her I suspect. She thinks she's getting away with it." He forced an unconvincing laugh.

"I'm grateful," Shawn lied. Honestly with the Black Foxes' blackmailing him, getting away from DOSA would've been preferable, but he was too tired to think of a reason why he couldn't stay at HQ.

It's not like I have a plan yet anyway—and even if I did, is that mind-reader tracking me? Is she listening to me right now?

"You okay?" Pangolin tilted his head to one side.

Realizing he was standing awkwardly, staring into the middle distance, Shawn shook himself out of it.

"Tired is all. Thanks for the room. Third floor?"

"Yep. Second door on the right, I believe."

"Thanks," Shawn said again before leaving the room and taking the stairs up two levels.

He shut himself into his room and sat on the end of the bed, not bothering to turn on the lights.

If I'm not safe in my own thoughts, how am I going to beat this? What are they even going to ask of me? What am I willing to do to save her?

The truth was a lot more than he should. Supervillains rarely went after non-DOSA family members for financial gain. There was an unspoken allowance for ultimate retribution if they did and with DOSA's strict policies against ransom and negotiation, there wasn't usually a benefit to it. That didn't mean the idea of his loved ones being in danger had never entered Shawn's mind, and Jules being an active hero made her position trickier. He'd cross almost any line to get her back.

I wish I could talk to Dad. They can't be listening in all the time, can they? How does that even work?

Mind reading was a super rare ability. He had heard of maybe two sables who claimed it—both of whom had been DOSA and one of whom was dead. Because of that, he wasn't exactly sure of the limitations it had.

He turned on the lights and found that his backpack had been placed beside the nightstand. Digging through this, he fished out a fresh T-shirt and boxers. A shower then rest. Maybe something would come to him in the morning.

Before he could enter the small bathroom attached to the room, his phone rang.

His heart stopped. Was it the Black Foxes?

He fumbled in his pocket and managed to get his phone out without dropping it. The caller ID read simply, "Katie."

His anxiety lessened somewhat. He answered. "Hi. Did you need anything?"

"Just checking in on you. I was hoping for an update. I'm guessing if you haven't sent one that means nothing's changed."

"Yeah." He moved into the bathroom and set his clothes beside the sink before kicking off his shoes and picking up the tiny bottle of hand lotion and the credit-card-sized, paper-wrapped bar of soap. Yeah, these had definitely come from a hotel.

"They don't have any leads. This group seems to be able to appear and disappear at a whim. Almost as if they're jumping through portals."

"Is that even possible? I mean, there's at least one hero with that power on the west coast. Porthole or something?"

"Porter." Shawn chuckled. "Though if I ever meet him, I'm totally calling him 'Porthole' now."

"You're so good at making friends. Do you think that's what's going on?"

"Unlikely. The ones we've seen have other powers and not ones I've ever seen combined with portal creation."

"Some sort of tech, then? DOSA has the gateway system, after all."

"Maybe, but ... I don't know. That would be a big leap forward. I hate to think they have access to something like that when we don't." He returned to sit on the edge of his bed, pulled off his socks, then flexed his toes against the short, commercial-grade carpet.

"I have a contact from the old days who might know. He's a tech guy my dad worked with sometimes. Should I reach out to him?"

Shawn hesitated. Did he want to draw Katie into this? She'd think it was suspicious if he turned down the offer of help, though. He needed to give the appearance that everything was normal. "I guess—but tell my dad you're doing it and don't agree to meet with anyone without backup, okay?"

"I'm not an idiot, Shawn," she said reproachfully.

More than he could say for himself.

"I know, I just worry … you're right. You're smart. You can handle yourself. My dad will help you, though. Please, give him a call."

"I will." There was a pause. Shawn wished he could crawl through the phone for a hug. He could use that right now—or just the chance to tell someone what was going on, but that might get Juliet killed. Why had he come here? He could be safe at home with his family right now. "How are the girls?" he asked, desperate to think about anything else.

"They're fine. Your mom took them to the Legoland Discovery Center today. Wore them both out, but they had a blast. Hana fell asleep right after her bath, and I put Evie down about fifteen minutes ago. She asked where you were."

"What did you tell her?" he asked.

"That you went to help Aunt Jules with something but would be home soon. She seemed to accept that."

"That's good. I wouldn't want them to worry."

Though what would he tell them if the worst happened? Hana might not be old enough to understand, but Evie would notice if her favorite aunt was never at Christmas again or didn't call her on her birthday or—

Shawn's will broke, and tears flooded his eyes. He choked back a sob.

"Shawn, are you okay?" Worry tainted Katie's voice.

"I'll … I'll be fine. I just … I love you, okay? And the girls. So much."

"I know," she soothed. "You're the best husband and father a woman could ask for. You'll get her back, Shawn. I feel it. It's almost like God's speaking to me, and maybe it's wishful thinking, but I have to believe He's got our back this time. For you and me, but also for Jules."

"I hope you're right," Shawn whispered. He hadn't even thought about prayer. Was his faith that unpracticed? That weak? "Will you pray with me? For me, too, but right now, with me?"

"Of course," she murmured.

Shawn closed his eyes and listened to her words. Maybe it was too much to hope for a miracle, but he could use one about now.

Chapter Nine

Juliet's eyes fluttered open, and she found herself staring across the room to where Sandstorm lay, stretched out on his cot. The green, military-style blanket covered most of him, but his sock-clad feet stuck out from one end, and his disheveled, sandy-brown hair peeked out from the other. His feet hung out a good deal over the edge of the cot, which didn't seem comfortable at all, but he'd said he was used to it.

She sat up and rubbed the sand out of her eyes. What was it now? Day four? Five? She needed some way to keep track. Maybe she should start scratching marks on the wall like a cartoon jailbird. The thought made her snort-laugh.

Sandstorm sat bolt upright, bleary-eyed. "Huh? Did you say something?"

"No." She stood. Her slightly too-large sweat pants slipped down her hips, so she pulled them up and yanked the drawstrings to cinch them about her waist. Even though she hadn't exposed more than a little midriff with the action, Sandstorm still averted his eyes.

Man, how did this guy end up as a villain? He obviously had some 'decent human being' trained into him at some point.

Mentallica—who Sandstorm had told her was named 'Danica' but never went by that—had loaned her two outfits. She'd need to either get another set or do some washing soon, but since she didn't do much more than sit in her room, they didn't get grimy. She'd set aside one set to be her designated "workout" clothes so she could do some cardio or body weight exercise. After a couple of sessions, those became super ripe, almost making her gag to put them on, but she needed to move to keep from going crazy. Also, she'd discovered a security camera in one of the vents. She'd covered it with a pillowcase, but the chances were high there were more spy cams she hadn't found. She wasn't going to risk nude Pilates or whatever just to keep her clothes unsweaty. She'd tried washing them in the sink with some of the men's body wash. It had kind of worked, but they hadn't dried right and still smelled musty.

Sandstorm sat on the edge of his cot and pulled his work boots on before picking up his leather jacket from the end of the bed and donning that.

"You want breakfast?" he asked.

"Yes, please." She nodded.

He ghosted around the door only to return a split second later, grimacing.

"What?" she asked.

"Diamondback is lurking down the hall. I don't want to deal with him right now." He pulled his cot away from the door. "Mind if I linger for a while?"

"No, that's okay." It wasn't as if she had a choice. What was she going to do if she didn't like him there? Leave?

"Thanks."

They sat in awkward silence for a moment.

"Is Diamondback still ticked off?" she asked. While Mentallica and Sandstorm took turns bringing her food and Sandstorm kept watch every night, she hadn't seen the other two members of the gang since her first day there.

"It's his default setting. I honestly can't remember a time he wasn't pissy about something." He scratched at his head, ruffling his hair. "Just so you know, he assumes I'm ... well, he knows I've been in here every night. In his head that means there's something going on with us. The idea that I'm getting 'benefits' he's denied—yeah, he's not happy about that."

Her face heated. Well, what did she care what villains thought about her love life? "Do you think ... I mean, he hasn't tried anything. Do you still need to stay here to protect me?"

"I'm not sure. I hope he's gotten it out of his system, but I'd hate to be wrong."

"Yeah." She'd hate for him to be wrong too.

Juliet bent down and fiddled with the disruptor cuff. She missed her powers so much. She hated feeling powerless. Kind of spoiled, she supposed. There were plenty of normies—including her sister and mother—who lived their whole lives without super abilities. Of course, they didn't get to be superheroes, but they also didn't get themselves captured by supervillains and cause their families to worry to death. Dang, if Abigail could see her now, she'd be so smug about it. Of course, Juliet would put up with that if it meant seeing her sister ... or her brother ... or mom, or dad, or little nieces ...

"You okay?" Sandstorm asked.

Tears spurted from her eyes and down her cheeks. Her insides squirmed.

"No. I'm a prisoner of supervillains with no hope of seeing the outside of this room again, let alone making it to my twenty-fourth birthday. Of course I'm not okay!" she snapped.

He crossed the room to stand over her. She avoided his gaze. "Yeah, but you've been that for five days now, and I've never seen you cry during it. Something set that off. Just sayin'."

She sniffled. "I was thinking about my family. They ... they're good people. We're close. I know they're worrying about me, and ... It sucks."

"Yeah, it does." He sat on the end of the bed, a good foot from her but still closer than he usually got. "You want to tell me about them? I know you have a dad and brother in DOSA."

Her eyes narrowed at him. "How do you know that?"

"It's public record." He shrugged. "You DOSA types don't exactly go for the secret identities. I've run into maybe two heroes in my career who couldn't be researched with a little bit of googling or what Mentallica calls 'social engineering.'"

Her chest tightened. Was he looking into her? Would he use it to get into her head? Mess with her?

"I saw you and your brother in an Instagram photo," he said. "Recognized him as kind of a DOSA rising star. Must run in the family."

"Compared to Shawn, I'm the screw-up of the family," she scoffed. "He's always been the golden boy, and I'm the wild child. Not that they don't love us all equally. Even Abigail who doesn't have powers, I don't think they ever made her feel like she wasn't still 'special,' but things just come easier for Shawn. He's got that charm, I guess. People like him. I'm a little abrasive."

"Really? Never would've guessed." He smirked.

She stuck her tongue out at him.

"Close family's a big deal. You're lucky to have that, and abrasive or not, they're lucky to have you. I'm sure they know that," he said.

Irritation flooded Juliet. She was giving him way too much of herself. Yeah, she'd been trying to get him to trust her, but that couldn't all be one way. She needed to turn things around and get something from him. She wasn't particularly good at vulnerability and touchy-feely stuff like that, but she could do humor. Maybe that would work.

"You know something about family, then? What's yours like? Does your mother know what you're doing, young man?" She peered down her nose at him in her best imitation of her mother.

"She's dead," he said simply.

"Oh." Her cheeks burned. She searched his face, hoping he was joking or lying. His expression remained inscrutable. "And the rest of your family?"

"Supervillainy isn't great for longevity," he said. "Both my parents were gone by the time I was two. My uncle took me in for a while, but he died when I was a teenager—also he was a sociopath, so I never got attached to him. Just because I didn't have what you do doesn't mean I can't see that it's a good thing, though." He focused on his hands, resting on his knees, for a moment, before speaking again. "You're ... you're the youngest, aren't you?"

"Yes. Shawn's four years older than me and Abigail is two. My parents believed in spacing." She laughed uncomfortably.

"Surge's baby sister," he mumbled.

"I guess." She frowned.

"There's a pretty big age gap between you two." His hand moved to his jacket pocket. She wondered what he kept in there and couldn't stop fiddling with. "Are you still close?"

"Well, yeah." The memory of her last conversation with Shawn, about his baby on the way, his concern for her safety, it gripped her by the heart and wouldn't let go. "We were two kids with superpowers. There weren't a lot of people in our peer group who understood that. He's the one who gave me my nickname, Jules, and who taught me how to cope when my powers manifested during middle school. I mean, Abigail is great. I love her, but it was Shawn who always looked out for me."

"I can see that." He stood. "You might see them again. Don't give up, okay?"

She wanted to snap at him again. After all, her situation sucked. With any other villain she'd have thought they were making fun of her, but Sandstorm—no, whatever he was, he wasn't needlessly cruel. She nodded, avoiding his eyes.

Sandstorm crossed to the door. "I'll be back with your breakfast."

"Thank you," she whispered.

As soon as he was gone, she entered the bathroom and leaned up against the sink. She couldn't count on his help getting her out of this. It was a good plan, but she needed a backup—and a backup to the backup, multiple backups and options. Her family and DOSA would be doing everything they could to get her back. She had to try and help them help her.

Step one, she needed to get out of the room. Ironically, Sandstorm making himself her primary caretaker made this harder. She could imagine standing by the door and knocking the others over the head with something when they entered, but Sandstorm never unlocked the door when he came in. He always used his powers to go through or around it. If she knocked him out, she'd still be stuck in here unless he happened to have something in his pockets she could use to get the door open. She wasn't going to leave that up to chance. Maybe if one of the others came to see her, she'd try it, though.

Since Sandstorm had taken his weights back, she'd need to find something else to use as a weapon. There was the top of the toilet tank. Heavy, unwieldy, and hard to hide, though. She'd have to have it already near the door when the person came though because there was no way she would have time to run, get it, and bash someone with it before they could walk through the door and see what she was up to. Something more portable that she could hide behind her back would be better.

Thinking this over, she brushed her teeth, washed her face, and combed out her dark hair with her fingers. This taken care of, she did what had to be her hundredth search of the room, but this time specifically looking for weapons.

She'd just pulled the mattress off the pallet bed to look under it when someone rapped on her door.

"It's me," Sandstorm called out.

"Hold on." She shoved the mattress back in place then

quickly changed shirts to make it look like she'd been undressed. "Okay, I'm decent now."

He filtered around the door and re-solidified with another paper bowl, presumably filled with oatmeal, in one hand and a paper plate with something yellow and lumpy looking on it. "We're down to just plain oatmeal." He set them both down on top of the bedside table. "I found some powdered eggs shoved in the back of the cabinet. I don't know if they're any good. They look—off."

"Food is food." She shrugged.

"Maybe this will help." He pulled a small bottle of hot sauce out of the inner pocket of his jacket and passed it to her. "I'll see you at dinner?"

"I'm not going anywhere." She sniffed.

He laughed before disappearing through the door again.

Juliet picked up the fork that lay next to the weird-looking eggs and poked at them before sprinkling the hot sauce generously on top and picking up the plate. A piece of folded paper sat under the plate. She hesitated. A note?

She took the piece of paper off the mattress. It was warm to the touch as if it had just come off an older style of printer. She unfolded it, and a lump formed in her throat. It was black and white and the resolution wasn't great, but it was still her family. She recognized the photo as the one they'd taken the previous Christmas, the last time they were all together. Mom, Dad, Shawn and his family, Abigail, and her. How had he gotten this? Oh, her Instagram. Of course. He'd gone out of his way to print it up for her?

Appetite gone, she sat on the edge of her bed and stared at the blurry image of everyone she loved. A tear dropped down and smeared the ink.

"I'm not going to stop fighting," she whispered. "I'm going to see you again. I promise."

Chapter Ten

Shawn wandered along a stretch of the riverside trail, his thoughts churning. It had been several days with no word from the villains who had his sister, and while he was grateful they had yet to make any demands of him, the silence was almost worse. How did he even know if she were still okay? Maybe they hadn't contacted him because something had happened to her and they'd lost their leverage. Maybe Shawn had done something wrong already, given them a reason to believe he wouldn't cooperate, and they'd decided to cut their losses and just —

He shuddered.

Ahead a couple of benches faced the river, so he jogged to one and sat down, staring out at the water.

Juliet's team had proven worse than useless. While he knew he shouldn't be so hard on them—it wasn't like he'd done any better—their complete lack of progress frustrated him. He needed this fixed before the Black Foxes forced his hand. If not ... it depended on their demands, he guessed. Maybe he could feed them some useless information and string them along until DOSA made some headway on the case. If not—if they wanted him to do something that would hurt people—would Juliet even want to be saved at that cost? She was as much a hero as he was. This career could mean paying the ultimate price. They both knew that.

Not like this, though. When I have a chance to save her—

His phone buzzed in his pocket and he pulled it out. *Katie.*

He looked around. There were a few joggers but all of

them appeared to be in their own worlds, most with earbuds in.

He answered the phone. "Hey."

"Hey yourself. Are you doing all right?"

He considered his response. "No, but that's to be expected. Still no sign of Juliet or the Black Foxes. We don't know where they're lairing or how they are traveling. For all we know they could be hiding within the city and we're just idiots."

"I might be able to help you with that." The smile in her voice made him sit up straighter.

"Your tech guy came through?"

"Yeah, he did. Your father is chasing it up the ladder to see if he can verify it though," she said.

"Up the ladder? Within DOSA?"

"That's the thing. When I talked to Jinxy, I could tell he knew what I was talking about, but he acted all suspicious, as if he thought I was trying to entrap him."

"Well, you are DOSA now, and you did say the guy was a contact from your villain days," Shawn pointed out.

"Yeah, but we parted on good terms. He even sent me a shower gift when Evie was born. It's one of her favorites."

Shawn thought for a moment. "Is that where the Totoro plush came from?"

"It was awful nice of him."

"How did he—" Shawn shut his mouth and pushed aside worries about this guy knowing their mailing address. "Never mind. So, he was suspicious?"

"Yeah, he seemed to think it was a trap from DOSA. It turns out, he'd heard rumors of that tech a few years ago, but it had been suppressed *by* DOSA. National security risk or something."

"Yeah, they can do that." He mulled over this for a moment. Dang it, he did not want to be dealing with more internal corruption. He'd seen enough of that in the agency for a lifetime. "You don't think they're DOSA, do you? Rogue agents?"

"No. I think they really are Black Foxes. Apparently when the scientist had his patent suppressed, he put his remaining prototypes up on the dark web for the highest bidder. No one knows who won the auction—"

"But the Black Foxes are a decent bet." Shawn massaged his forehead, trying to ward off a growing headache. "So does that help us at all?"

"Maybe? If DOSA has the schematics they probably know the range and limitations. It might help narrow down possible search areas?"

"Yeah, it could—" Shawn hesitated. What if the villains were listening in on him somehow right now? He cast an anxious glance around but only saw more joggers. Of course, there was a chance they'd hacked his phone—

I'm getting paranoid. I can't stop investigating without DOSA getting suspicious though. They have to see that.

Shawn tensed, suddenly feeling like a goldfish under the eyes of a cat. He couldn't get away. His phone, his private conversations, even his own thoughts were potentially exposed, and he had nowhere to hide.

What am I going to do? I need to do something...

"Babe, are you still there?" Katie's voice brought him back to the present.

"Uh, yeah, just thinking. It sounds like Dad's chasing down the lead?"

"Yeah, he said he'd look into it and if he found anything, forward it to Juliet's team leader."

"That's good." Shawn stood. "Thanks for the update, Katie. I love you."

"I love you too. Stay safe."

"Okay," he murmured. He hung up the phone. His only hope was finding out where Juliet was being held and saving her himself. That had to be his next step. He wasn't going to sit and wait any longer.

Chapter Eleven

Juliet stretched into a downward dog then up into a cobra pose, trying to keep her mind clear. Yoga wasn't her favorite, but it took focus, and she needed something to concentrate on other than her barely-formed escape plans. She counted breaths as she held the pose, savoring the tightness in her muscles but the openness of her chest. Deep breath in, deep breath out ...

Someone knocked on the door.

"Dinner time," Sandstorm called out.

She hopped up. She must've lost track of time. Not that it was ever easy to count hours here.

"Come in."

He filtered through the door carrying another paper plate with a basic white bread sandwich.

"Same as yesterday?" she asked.

"It's all we have left." He passed her the plate.

Not hungry yet and not appetized by the idea of another bland sandwich, she set it on the small table next to her bed.

"After tonight, we'll have more options," he said. "Diamondback and Mentallica are making a supply run. We'll be rolling in Doritos soon enough."

"Part of a balanced breakfast, I'm sure." She clicked her tongue. "Are you villains or college freshmen?"

"Living our best life, either way." He winked.

The rasp of the deadbolt scraping open spun Sandstorm around. Juliet's lower lip went slack when Diamondback stepped in, sneering at Sandstorm.

"What are you doing in here?" Sandstorm demanded.

"Easy. I could ask the same of you." Diamondback addressed Sandstorm, but his eyes flitted past him to slide over Juliet. Her skin crawled. "Wallace told me you're not coming along on the supply run. Why?" He came within arm's reach of Sandstorm.

"I have work to do." Sandstorm's form shimmered, hinting that he'd activated his powers. The difference between him being solid and when he'd faded but had yet to break into a cloud was subtle, like a slight haze where the outlines of his body were blurred.

"Work or play?" Diamondback's gaze cut to Sandstorm. "Seems like you're spending a lot of time with our 'prisoner.' Why don't you go on the supply run with Mentallica and let me take a turn watching out for this cutie?" He dipped his head in Juliet's direction.

"No thanks," Juliet said.

"No one asked you." Diamondback's lips curled, and he stepped through Sandstorm to stand in front of Juliet.

"I'm warning you, Huxley," Sandstorm said. "Back off."

Diamondback waved dismissively and continued to leer at Juliet.

Juliet stared Diamondback straight in the eye. Even without her abilities, she wasn't going to let him intimidate her.

"I shouldn't be surprised you're keeping this little thing all to yourself." Diamondback kept his eyes on Juliet. "I guess having dead parents, you never learned to share your toys."

He reached towards her face, and instinctively her left arm rose into a block and her right fist rocketed towards his chin. He dodged. Her blow went high, grazing across his teeth. A stinging pain cut through her, and she fell back, staring at a thin scrape across her knuckles, red blood beading.

"Cut it out!" Sandstorm pushed Diamondback to the side and stood between them.

Diamondback wiped at his mouth, his snake-like fangs dripping. "That wasn't very smart, sweetheart."

The stinging pain in Juliet's hand spread down her arm, and her fingers tingled and went numb. Cold fear swept through her. What had she done?

"Get out of here!" Sandstorm barked.

Diamondback snickered. "She has a chance. I didn't intend to bite her, so she didn't get a full dose. You never know how it'll go down, though. Sometimes a drop is enough." He strode out of the room.

Sandstorm took a step towards him as if to follow before grunting, slamming the door shut, and hurrying into the bathroom.

She gripped her right wrist with her unharmed left hand. It was barely a scratch. How bad could it be?

Sandstorm returned, now carrying the first aid kit from the bathroom.

"Can I see?" He motioned towards her hand.

She offered it to him. He pushed her sweatshirt sleeve up to her elbow then wound a snake bite bandage around her arm.

"What ... what's going to happen?" she stammered.

"I'm not sure," he murmured. "Maybe nothing. He didn't actually bite you, so it might not be enough venom to do any damage. Even with a full dose—well, it's not a hundred percent—"

"What percentage is it?" she asked.

He hesitated.

"I'm a big girl, Sandy, but I need to know my chances. Have you seen him bite before? Is it deadly?"

"Yeah, we did a heist together right after he joined our team," Sandstorm said. "Like I said, it's not a hundred percent. It takes a few days for his venom to recharge so he doesn't always use enough to kill even when he's in full attack mode. Sometimes just incapacitate. That said, some people are more susceptible than others. It was an incidental dosage. Plus you're a sable. Your healing factor should help."

"Sure..." She still couldn't feel her fingers, and her

hand had turned red. Of course, that might be the effects of the bandage cutting off her circulation. "So it's either nothing because he didn't dose me high enough or ... I might die?"

"I think if he'd given you enough to kill you we'd be seeing more of a reaction already." He searched her face. "Any symptoms?"

"I can't feel my hand." She nodded down to her bandaged limb.

His lips pursed. "Not great, but also not terrible. No nausea? Any pain? Lightheadedness? Blurred vision?"

"I feel a little dizzy, but that might be adrenaline fading," she said. "Are those all the symptoms?"

"A strong dose, you might get some hallucinations or lose consciousness, but this was incidental, so I don't think that'll be an issue." He glanced at the door. "Look ... I think you'll be fine, but I want to keep an eye on you. Just in case you have some sort of delayed reaction."

"Sure," she said slowly. "So you're going to sit in here and stare at me ... again?"

"No. I have assigned duties today," he said. "You're going to have to accompany me."

"Out of my cell? Is your boss going to be okay with that?"

"You've got a disruptor on. Plus if she asks, it was Diamondback's fault." He motioned to her bare feet. "You might want to grab some socks. The floors can be cold."

She fetched a pair of socks and sat on the edge of the bed, fumbling in an attempt to get them on one-handed.

"Want some help?" he asked.

Her mouth twisted. No. She wanted to do this herself, but dang, it was a lot harder than she thought it would be.

"Yeah, I guess," she mumbled.

Her breath hitched as he knelt in front of her. She handed him the socks, and he slipped them over each foot in turn.

He laughed. "You've got tiny feet, Cinderella."

She wrinkled her nose at him. "Cinderella? I prefer short stuff if those are my choices."

He guffawed, and she found herself smiling in spite of her nerves.

Socks on, she stood but immediately wobbled. The world spun.

He gripped her arm. "Are you okay?"

She drew several deep breaths before the room steadied. "Yeah, I'll be fine. I think I stood up too fast."

He searched her face, and she had to look away. "I'll be fine."

"You better be. I wouldn't want to lose a valuable asset."

She considered him. His expression remained serious. Was that a joke? Or did he still see her that way? She'd hoped she'd been breaking through his barriers. Her whole "gain his trust" strategy was based on it.

He's still a villain. I can't trust him, and I can't let myself think he trusts me until I'm absolutely sure.

He led her from the room, shutting the door behind them. "We'll take the elevator."

Juliet's legs felt weak, her extremities unnaturally cool, but she was uncertain whether that was the effects of Diamondback's venom or just her own fear. When they entered the elevator, she leaned against the wall, trying to focus on anything other than what had happened.

Sandstorm eyed her.

"I'm fine." She frowned. "I'll tell you if it gets worse. Stop watching me like a time bomb."

"Sorry." The elevator door dinged open, and he motioned to her. "Ladies first."

They were on the second level, the one with the command center with all the computers. He took her past this, however, into the room she'd originally teleported into, a mostly empty space with the same flickering lights that lit the whole lair. With more time to look around now, she examined the area. There were lots of metal drawers in the wall, each with a keypad lock, and many crates of what she assumed were supplies and equipment. No door besides the one they'd entered from, leading into the lair.

"This is where you port in and out of, right? What are we doing here?"

"Maintenance." He walked to one of the drawers. He entered the code quickly, but she still caught it: one, one, five, six. She committed this to memory.

Careless of you, Sandy.

She eased closer to him. Two metal briefcases sat inside, the heavy-duty kind. Sandstorm opened the first, revealing a series of teleportation disks resting in black foam. There were six disks left with four empty spaces, suggesting the case had originally held ten.

"We're running lower than I'd like," he said

"What do you need to do with them? Make more?" she asked.

"Nah. I mean, it would be nice if I could, but I can't." He slid aside a panel at the bottom of the drawer revealing a series of cords that ran into the wall. "They lose charge over time. We have to make sure they're refueled, so to speak." One by one he picked up the teleportation disks, plugged them into charge cords, and set them back down.

Juliet bit her bottom lip. Those disks could be her way out of this. Could she overcome Sandstorm and take one? Definitely not without a weapon of some sort. Even with a weapon, he could ghost and let the blow go right through him unless she managed to get a good, hard hit on him before he saw her coming. Unlikely, but if the chance came up—

Trying not to be too obvious, she scanned the area for something that would make a good club.

"I thought they drew power from their surroundings," she said, hoping if she kept him distracted with conversation he wouldn't watch her too carefully. "When you used them back in Pittsburgh, they made the lights flicker."

"Oh, they do draw what they can from their surroundings, but they take so much power they also need a supplementary source, so we keep them charged at all times. Plus you can't be sure the area you need to port in and out of will have enough power sources for your trip." He double-checked all the cords.

"How far is the range on those?" she asked.

"Wouldn't you like to know?" He looked over his shoulder at her. "I suppose you want me to give you a lesson in how to use them too. Should I give you the keys to the place while I'm at it?"

"Whatever," she muttered. "Villains are idiots."

Sandstorm arched an eyebrow. "Why do you say that?"

"You own teleportation tech that could change the world. That's got to be worth more as a legitimate business than you could ever hope to make with your dumb villain schemes." She crossed her arms over her chest.

"You're assuming we didn't steal this tech too."

She eyed him. "Did you?"

"Sort of." He held up one of the disks. "DOSA actually owns the patents. Well, that is to say, they confiscated the rights and suppressed the information under some sort of national security BS when a private citizen tried to patent them. We managed to get a hold of the prototypes, but if someone tried to manufacture the tech legally, DOSA would shut them down." He plugged it in and put it down again. "They're expensive to make, though. Too expensive for them to hand out to their lackeys. My understanding is they only use them for top secret ops that you low-level types aren't high enough clearance to be in on."

Juliet bristled. "I'm not a low-level—"

"Yeah, short stuff, you are, and not just height-wise."

He chuckled.

She stuck her chin in the air, irritated at the thought of her agency keeping secrets from her that random villains knew about somehow.

"We also only got the prototypes, not the schematics, so we really can't make more once the ones we have are gone. Even if we could, I don't think Wallace would want to risk our rivals getting a hold of the tech. She's not into sharing power." His face grew grave. "That's kind of part of the villain package."

"Speaking of Wallace, where is she?" Juliet looked around.

"Her quarters, probably. She doesn't really like to associate with the rest of us, so she'll lock herself in there for hours. She has cameras she can use to watch the whole lair from her phone." He pulled out the second of the two briefcases and opened it up. His brow furrowed.

"What is it?" Juliet came to stand next to him. The case in front of him had the same two rows of five, except this case only had one missing.

"We're short one." He tapped his fingers on the edge of the case before beginning his task and plugging these in as well. "We keep a pretty strict inventory on these. They're only good for a handful of transports each before their power element burns out. Someone took one—and recently. I just got in here a few days ago to issue Mentallica the one she's using on the supply run."

Juliet leaned over the case, one eye on Sandstorm in case he tried to stop her. The disks had a single dial in the center. There were multiple settings it could be switched to. The one at the bottom was labeled "home" and each other setting was just a number. Places they could port to, maybe? That wasn't great. Even if she did get a hold of one, it would be a matter of luck where she'd end up. Not ideal, but anywhere would be better than here.

Before she could move, Sandstorm gave the drawer a push, and it slid shut with a whir and a click.

Chance gone. Probably wouldn't have been able to fight him, though. Not without my powers.

She poked at the disruptor anklet with the toes of her opposite foot. There had to be a way to get that thing off.

"So where did it go?" Sandstorm mused.

"Don't look at me. This is the first time I've been out of my cell in over a week."

"Didn't say you took it." His gaze fell on her arm. "You seem to be doing all right."

She swallowed. She hadn't even thought about her injury since he'd brought her here. If she admitted to feeling better already, would he shove her back in her cell? She had so much more intelligence to gather.

"I'm ... not bad. Just a little dizzy." She swayed then braced herself against the wall, letting out a slight whimper. "Maybe I should sit down?"

The corners of his mouth twitched. "Think you can walk down the hall? I want to check the security feeds."

"I ... might be able to manage." She peeled herself off the wall.

"So brave of you," he deadpanned.

She followed him down the hall to the command center. Once inside, he pointed to a chair in the corner.

"Sit."

Her chest heated. "I'm not a dog."

"Sorry. Please sit there. Is that better?"

She didn't move.

"Okay, look. I'm already pushing it having you out of your cell," he said. "If Wallace checks the security feeds and sees I'm letting you sit close enough to our computer system to push buttons, she'll crush my skull like popping a balloon."

Juliet hesitated. Yeah, she was here to gain intel, but she was also only out of her cell due to him. He could just as easily put her back. She sat.

"Wallace would crush you? She doesn't seem that scary. What are her powers?"

"Telekinesis, but she can move more with her mind than most strength sables can with their arms." Sandstorm took a seat in front of one of the computers and typed in a password with two fingers.

A few clicks later and he was browsing through file folders. "K, so I know it was after I gave Mentallica her disk, so after ... this ... still a lot of footage to cover." He let out a low whistle. For the next several minutes, Sandstorm pulled up video files and fast-forwarded through them,stopping and watching at regular speed if someone entered the room.

After a bit, Juliet risked scanning the area. There were several monitors, but all appeared to be locked.

They have to be monitoring the bombs remotely, and it would make sense for the access point to be these computers. If only I could get a good look at them.

"Yep. I thought so," Sandstorm said suddenly.

She craned her neck to watch. He'd paused on a frame of Diamondback bending over the now open portal disk drawer.

"He's stealing them?" She came to look over his shoulder. He didn't tell her to sit back down. "Why?"

"Watch and see." He scrolled forward a few frames. Diamondback stepped through a portal and disappeared.

"Where's he going? What could be important enough to risk stealing from his own gang?" Juliet asked.

"I have a guess." Sandstorm continued to fast-forward before another blue portal opened up and Diamondback returned, clutching a brown paper bag. "Dang him."

"Booze?" Juliet asked. "All this for a drink?"

"Yep. He's an idiot with no self-control." Sandstorm made a copy of the video file and pulled up an email application. "Going to let Wallace know and then search out where he's hiding it. He's too much of a wildcard when he drinks. We can't risk that so close to a mission."

"How'd he get away with it, though?" Juliet frowned.

"He didn't," Sandstorm pointed out. "I just caught

him."

"That's not what I mean. You have that mind reader popping in and out of your heads. Wouldn't she have caught onto his plan or realized that he's hiding something?"

"Mentallica? Not really. Her powers don't work that way. Yeah, you have to be careful around her, but she's not that hard to get around."

"Seriously? She makes me feel like she can read all my thoughts! I can't imagine anything more violating." Juliet shuddered. "I must be an open book to her. She probably even knows about the *My Little Pony* fanfic I wrote in middle school."

"As curious as I now am about your fanfics, it's not that tough," he said. "Most sables don't know how to deal with mind readers simply because they haven't encountered them, but they're not all-powerful. Without a lot of effort, they can only read what you're thinking at any given moment, so if you keep your immediate thoughts under control, you won't have any problems."

"Isn't that kind of like telling someone not to think about elephants?" She frowned.

"It takes practice, sure, but it's doable. That's not the important question though." He eyed her. "I'm guessing you're a Rainbow Dash girl. You seem the type."

She stuck her tongue out at him. He chose another video clip and scanned forward a bit, hopping through several different security feeds to trace Diamondback's path down the hall and into the elevator. On the lower level, Diamondback disappeared into another room.

"What's in there?" she asked.

"Break room." His mouth wrinkled. "There are only a handful of rooms in this lair that aren't covered by cameras, and that's one of them." He closed the video files then selected the menu option to put the computer back to sleep. As he did, she noted a folder on the desktop labeled "targets." That was what she needed—if she could only get to it.

He stood. "Come on. I want to have that bottle dumped before he gets back, and supply runs don't take that long."

Juliet followed him into the break room. It wasn't much. A small kitchenette with some basic appliances and a cheap-looking table with three chairs around it. Apparently this team didn't eat together all that often. Of course, she wouldn't want to eat with Diamondback. His table manners would probably be atrocious.

"Want to earn some brownie points?" Sandstorm asked. "There's a lot of cabinets to go through. Going to help me search?"

She opened her mouth for a retort then a thought struck her. She might find something useful in one of these cabinets. "Sure," she said, walking to the closest one and opening it up.

So that's where they keep the dang oatmeal.

She pushed aside the box of oatmeal packets and searched behind it.

"I personally like mine cold." Sandstorm opened the freezer. "Of course, I'm more of a beer man. You?"

"I'd kill for a nice margarita right now." She sighed. "Or anything lime flavored, really. Heck, I'd take a Sprite."

"Always a classic." He pulled several ice packs out of the way to search the very back of the freezer.

Juliet moved down the cabinets. A lot of them were empty. She found some scattered canned goods and cleaning supplies but no booze and nothing she could use as a weapon. On a whim, she opened the dishwasher.

"Really?" Sandstorm asked.

"You never know." She knelt next to it, and her breath caught in her chest. A steak knife stuck out of the silverware caddy on the bottom shelf. She glanced at Sandstorm, but his head was stuck in the fridge now, and he didn't seem to be paying attention to her. The knife wasn't very long but seemed sharp enough.

I'll only get one chance at this. I need to use it well.

Quickly she slipped it up her sleeve, blade first so she could grip the handle in her hand. The snake bite bandage protected her arm but also made her movements awkward. Still, probably better than using her left hand. She continued to search, or at least go through the motions of searching. It wasn't that hard. The next few cabinets were empty, with nothing to even move or look behind. Sandstorm finished his fridge investigation and got down on his knees to look under the sink. She eased closer to him, her grip sweaty on the knife hilt. One hit. If he saw her coming, he'd activate his powers, and she wouldn't get another shot.

She'd need to move quickly. One swift movement to get the knife out of her sleeve and into his body. Sandstorm's head and shoulders had disappeared beneath the sink. She plotted her attack. Between the ribs would be ideal, but easy to miss. The gut then? Unlikely to be an immediate kill—

An image of him, wounded, staring up at her, flashed through her brain followed by a memory of him standing guard over her only the night before, protecting her from Diamondback. Her determination faltered.

"Got it!" He announced triumphantly.

She forced her face out of its gape as he dragged a half-full handle of off-brand booze out from under the sink.

"He's gone through a lot in a few days," she managed to keep her voice from quavering even as her stomach roiled from self-doubt and self-reproach. How had she chickened out? He was a supervillain! Her captor! The enemy—

But he was also "Sandy," the one person who had shown her any kindness over the last week or so, the one person who had stood between her and death multiple times.

Still a bad move. I need to escape. It's my duty to escape. What sort of a hero am I?

Sandstorm set the bottle on the counter beside the sink, unscrewed the top, and sniffed it.

"Pugh. He went for the cheap stuff." He opened the cabinet above the sink and took out a plastic cup which he poured some of the drink into before holding it under his nose and then taking a sip. He coughed. "He's not drinking this for the taste for sure."

"What? You aren't into the delightful notes and subtle aftertaste of trash water?" she asked.

"Apparently not." His eyes twinkled. "You want a shot before I dump it out?"

"Trying to get me drunk, Sandy?" she asked.

"Nah, I wouldn't dare. It's probably a bad idea anyway. A little thing like you? This rot gut would knock you over," he teased.

She grabbed the bottle by the neck and threw back a swig.

It singed her throat as it went down, almost choking her, but she kept her expression stoic and maintained eye contact.

His eyes widened. "Careful, short stuff. You're pushing it for your weight class."

She slammed the bottle back down. "I can handle it."

He laughed and tipped the bottle into the sink. As the liquid glugged down the drain and his attention was diverted, Juliet braced herself against the kitchen counter, her head spinning.

On an empty stomach ... dumb, that was dumb.

She tightened her hold on the knife again, trying to keep it from cutting her arm beneath her sleeve. Today was a day for bad decisions, it seemed.

Sandstorm stepped back from the sink. "Well, that's done." He eyed her. "You don't seem to be dying from your snake-in-the-grass bite. Can I check your arm?"

Juliet's adrenaline spiked. Thinking quickly, she used

her left hand to grip the knife beneath her sleeve and pull it up her arm as she rolled up her sweatshirt to expose the snake-bite bandage and her grazed knuckles, already scabbed over.

"Yeah, you look fine," he said. "Try to move your fingers."

She clenched and unclenched her fist several times. "Yeah, I feel fine."

"Yep. Looks like I dragged you around the lair for nothing. Sorry about that. Let's get you back to your cell." He stepped back and waved towards the door. "Ladies first."

"Whatever." She eased the sleeve back in place and clutched the knife against her bandage again.

Still feeling lightheaded from her ill-advised swig, she followed him down the hall towards her room. As they were approaching the door, the elevator at the end of the hall slid open, and Diamondback stormed out.

Sandstorm pushed her forward and opened the door to the room. "Get in. Quick."

She stepped in front of him but paused when it didn't seem like he was going to follow. "You should—"

"Lucas!" Diamondback roared.

"I said, get in—" Sandstorm tried to force her into her room, but as his hand touched her, Diamondback collided with him. Sandstorm ghosted, causing Diamondback to go through him and hit the door frame, but also allowing Juliet to escape his grasp.

Diamondback whirled around, blocking the entrance to the room.

Sandstorm's jaw clenched. He grabbed Juliet's shoulders, and his energy prickled through her.

"It's too late," he said. "I already found your stash and dumped it. If you return the disk you stole, Wallace will go easy on you. We're too late in the game to hire replacement muscle."

Diamondback's face reddened and a Y-shaped vein

popped out in his forehead. "You snitch! You couldn't let it lie, could you? Had to go sticking your nose in my business—"

"My business is anything that could endanger the mission," Sandstorm said.

The elevator dinged, drawing Diamondback's eye. Juliet had just enough time to see Wallace step off the elevator before Sandstorm yanked her into the room, walking right through Diamondback.

Juliet stumbled back as he released her. She clutched the knife. Would she have time to draw it if this turned into a fight? Or any chance against multiple supervillains? Diamondback took a threatening step into the room. She held her breath.

"Lucas isn't the one you should be worried about, Huxley." Wallace followed Diamondback. "You violated several of my commands. If we weren't so close to the mission's end, I'd personally deal with you, but as is, just be happy you're not losing anything more than a quarter of your share."

Diamondback's jaw dropped. "A quarter? That wasn't the deal!"

"The deal was that you wouldn't do anything stupid and would obey my orders until we all got paid." Wallace's eyes flashed. "I'm within my rights to take everything from you, but I'm fair—"

"Fair?" Diamondback's lips curled back to reveal his glistening fangs.

Juliet's heart rose into her throat. Sandstorm's face remained placid. Maybe he was right not to be freaking out. After all, they had Diamondback outnumbered.

"Yes, you've made things more difficult for the rest of us and cost us several teleportation charges with your idiocy," Wallace continued. "I can't allow you to put the mission at risk—"

"Me? Put the mission at risk? I just wanted a drink!" Diamondback jabbed his finger at Sandstorm. "What about him?"

Sandstorm stood straighter.

"Sandstorm hasn't—"

"Like hell he hasn't!" Diamondback shouted. "He goes off on his own, claiming he's 'checking' on the devices, and we lose one. He drags this DOSA brat back here and convinces us to keep her alive because he's got some master plan. Well, I haven't seen any good coming of keeping her around. All he's done is cozy up with her every night—"

Juliet's face warmed.

"Look." Sandstorm took a step closer to Diamondback, though his body still shimmered, suggesting his powers were up. "You don't have to like me and I sure as hell don't have to like you, but we have a job to do—"

"Yeah, sure, that's all you care about." Diamondback spat. His spittle flew through Sandstorm as if he wasn't even there. It sizzled when it hit the floor. Juliet cringed.

"That's enough, Huxley," Wallace said. "We're done here. Out. Both of you."

The two men exchanged a spite-filled glance.

"You first." Sandstorm nodded towards the door.

"Why? You afraid to leave me alone with your plaything for a few seconds?" Diamondback sneered. He took a step towards her. "How's your hand, sweetheart? Want a matching one for the right side?"

Juliet squared her shoulders, her mind focused on the knife in her grip.

"Wallace said we're leaving." Sandstorm grabbed Diamondback by the shoulder and yanked him towards the door.

Diamondback hissed, lunged, and sank his fangs into Sandstorm's wrist. Sandstorm gasped and fragmented, causing Diamondback to stumble through him.

"Sandy!" Juliet gasped.

Chapter Twelve

Juliet's heart stopped. The outline of Sandstorm's body went hazy as if he were about to break into a cloud then formed solid again. He hit his knees, gripping an ugly-looking red wound on his arm.

Diamondback stood over him, smirking.

"What did you do?" Wallace roared.

Diamondback flew backwards, straight into the wall. He crashed into it and slid down onto his butt.

Wallace stormed over to stand above Sandstorm even as Juliet scrambled towards him. The villain boss raised her hand, and Juliet felt an invisible hand grip her by the front of her sweatshirt.

"How much did you give him?" Wallace asked.

Diamondback wheezed then glared at her. "As much as I could. Why? What are you going to do about it? Sandstorm's an idiot, but he was right: you can't afford to lose me as muscle right now. Especially if you're already going to be down one man." He staggered to his feet. "Looks like my share just got bigger."

Sandstorm drew several ragged breaths. Juliet stumbled for the bathroom. Knowing it wouldn't do any good with the current emergency, she stashed the knife at the back of the cabinet beneath the sink before snatching up the first aid kit and rushing out to Sandstorm again.

"I have ... let me help him!" she stammered.

Wallace nodded slowly. "Diamondback, out!"

Diamondback swaggered out the door, making Juliet wish that she'd held onto the knife. As soon as he was gone, Wallace stepped back, allowing Juliet access to Sandstorm.

The young villain's face had already gone gray and

sweat beaded on his brow. Juliet helped him remove his leather jacket to give her easier access to his arm. Diamondback's fangs had sunk in then raked across his inner arm, causing two deep punctures that tapered into jagged gashes.

"I've got you," she whispered, touching the side of his face. She did her best to copy what he'd done with her injury, though admittedly his was so much worse.

"It doesn't matter," Wallace said calmly. "With a full dose, that will at best delay things."

Sandstorm swallowed, his gaze rising to his boss's, though he didn't speak.

"You can't let him die!" Juliet snarled.

"He has maybe a twenty percent chance." Wallace shrugged. "I'm being generous because he's young, has a large body mass, and a strong sable healing factor. I once saw him recover from a broken arm in less than two weeks. Good rate even for a sable."

"You need to get him to a hospital! Or ... I don't know, do you villains even have doctors?"

"Can't risk having him outside the lair right now. Especially not incapacitated." Wallace went to the door. "Maybe you'll sweat it out, Lucas. I wish you the best, but you understand the business. Like I said earlier, if you and Huxley kill each other, well, that's a larger percentage for me."

"Got it," Sandstorm said through clenched teeth.

"Looks like you've got yourself a nurse for the night at least." She eyed Juliet who glowered at her. "Good luck." She left, closing the door behind her.

Juliet winced as the deadbolt slid into place. They were seriously going to leave him?

Sandstorm drew a deep breath, and she focused on him again. "Are you okay?"

He snorted. "No."

She bit her bottom lip. Maybe she should be glad this was happening. She hadn't had the nerve to stab him in the kitchen but this was karma, right? After all, he was a supervillain and the man holding her captive and ...

He doubled over. "Looks like you're stuck with me ... oh, man ... dang ..." He gripped his wrist below the wound then forced a laugh. "It kind of stings." His fake smile wavered, his hazel eyes watering.

Her chest cracked open. "What can I do to help?"

"Not ... much. Is it ... where's my cot? I need to lie down."

"You barely fit on that thing. Here. Lean on me." She slipped her arm around his chest.

"I don't think that's a good idea." He did his best to stand on his own, wavered, and bumped into her. She wobbled but braced herself and managed to keep them both standing. Oof, he was heavy.

"It's only a few feet. Come on." She helped him limp to her bed where he collapsed. He lay on his side then curled up into a fetal position.

"Let me get your shoes off," she said.

"Wait," he stammered, rolling over to look at her. "In the pocket of my jacket, there's a bottle cap."

"A bottle cap?" She frowned.

"Yes, please. I ... I want it."

Juliet hurried to rummage through his pockets, finding a few zip ties, the wrapper of a granola bar, a multi-tool, and finally a smooth metal disk. Quickly checking to see if he was looking and finding his eyes squeezed shut, she pocketed the zip ties and the multi-tool before taking the disk. It had obviously once been a bottle cap, but it was flattened and smoothed, with all the paint worn off. She brought it to him. He closed his hand around it and gripped it to his heart.

"What's so important about that thing?" she asked.

"It's a memory," he mumbled.

She returned to the foot of the bed and managed to get his shoes off.

"Juliet." His quavering voice grabbed her by the

throat, and she came to sit by his side.

"What?"

His lips pursed, the lines around his eyes deepening. "You're in pain?" she pushed.

"Yeah, but that's not—" He pried his eyes open. "If this goes ... if I don't make it through this, you need to get out of here. I won't ... I don't trust any of them with you. They'll kill you. Maybe not immediately, but soon. If I'm not here—you need to escape."

She swallowed. "Sandy, if I knew how to escape, don't you think I would've already?"

His mouth crinkled as if he'd tasted something bitter.

She gripped his uninjured hand. "How about you don't die and leave me alone, all right? Get through this for me."

"I'll try." He grimaced. "Oof. My head hurts—"

"There's some Advil in the first aid kit," she said. "Would that help?"

"Maybe? I'm not sure how it would interact with the venom. It's not like they do drug trials with villain powers." He laughed bitterly. "Maybe it's for the best. It'll help me stay awake. I'm ... it's a fight."

"Is it like a concussion? Where you aren't supposed to fall asleep?"

"Not really. At least I don't think so." He tried to sit up, but she put her hand on his chest and pushed him down. In spite of his advantages in size and strength, he didn't resist.

"Then why not sleep? Maybe it will help your body heal, and you won't be in pain."

"I'm ... I'm afraid I won't wake up," he whispered. He met her stare, his eyes intense, and for once she noticed how young he looked. His height and confidence masked it, but he had to be around her age, maybe even younger. "Look, I'm not afraid to die. Not really. It's always a looming threat with this job but—I don't want to die alone. Please, stay with me." His hands shook, whether from fear or the effects of the venom she couldn't be sure.

"I won't leave you," she soothed. "I'll stay and do whatever you need me to do. Just get through this."

A faint smile crossed his face before he shuddered again. "I'm sorry. Juliet, if you ... there's something ..." His eyes fell shut. "I'm ... what ... man ..." He trailed off.

"Sandy?" She rested her hand against his forehead. His skin was hot to the touch, and her hand came away damp with sweat. Her stomach twisted. "Please be okay. Don't leave me alone here."

He stirred but didn't open his eyes.

Juliet paced the room, stopping to check his pulse every so often. It beat faster than she thought it should, but she wasn't exactly a doctor. For all she knew he had a super high resting heart rate. Sable physiology could be weird sometimes.

Her stomach growled after a while. No one brought her food, but the sandwich from lunch still sat on the bedside table. Even as hungry as she was, it wasn't very appetizing, but she forced it down.

Sandstorm groaned in his sleep and rolled over. His T-shirt clung to his chest and shoulders, dampened by sweat. She hesitated. He'd get cold soon, but he'd fallen asleep on top of the blankets. She tried to pull them out from under him only to find him too heavy. Thankfully he had a blanket he used with his cot folded up in the corner. She draped it over his body.

Okay, God, if You're out there, can I ask for a favor? Things have been pretty lousy for me lately, but that is admittedly kind of my own fault—but he wouldn't be hurt if he hadn't stood up for me. Villain or not, I owe him my life. Don't let him die to protect me. Please. I don't want to be here alone.

She hadn't really expected an answer, but the silence still weighed on her. She brushed her fingers through his hair. It felt softer than she expected, and she found herself repeating the action.

The lights dimmed as they did every night. No one came to check in on her or him. Bored and wiped out from the stressful day, she set up his cot a couple of feet from her bed. She slipped off her socks then hesitated. The cot didn't look comfortable and with him using the blanket, it'd be cold. Also, he'd said he didn't want to be left alone.

She turned off the lights and came to stand over him. He'd curled up right on the edge of the bed and the mattress was a double. She'd definitely fit. She probably wouldn't even have to touch him. Plus, it'd be warm.

Pushing aside her last uncertainty, she lay beside him and pulled on the blanket to get it over both their bodies.

He shifted, his weight dipping the mattress and drawing her closer to him. She put her hand on his upper back. He moaned.

"It's okay," she soothed. "You're not alone."

He grew still again.

She lay there for several minutes, feeling the rise and fall of his ribs against her hand, before her eyes fell shut and she gave in to sleep.

A cry jerked her to consciousness what felt like moments later. She sat up and found him shaking. A seizure? No, the movement seemed more like he was trying to escape something.

"Easy, easy!" She brushed her hand against his cheek. "Sandy, are you okay?"

"M ... mom?" he stuttered.

She paused. Hadn't he said that he didn't have any family?

"No, it's ..." Realizing the futility of correcting a delirious man, she pulled her sleeve up over her hand so she could wipe the sweat from his brow again. His fever must've broken as his skin was now cold to the touch, maybe why he'd been shaking. That had to be a good sign, though, didn't it?

She brushed his hair back from his face. "It's okay. You're going to be okay."

"I'm trying ... I promise I'm trying, Mom. I won't leave ... I won't leave the path. I swear."

Leave the path?

"I know you won't," she said, even though she had no idea what he was talking about. Considering how out of it he was, maybe he didn't either.

"I promise, but it's so hard ... it ... it's..." He fell silent but continued to shiver. She slid down again and rested her hand on his side. He did feel cold. They needed more blankets ... or body heat.

She eased closer. He lay on his stomach so she ended up cuddled up against his side. Slipping one arm around his waist, she nestled her cheek against his back. He continued to shake for a moment before quieting again. With her body pressed against his, he began to warm. Heat circulated from her to him, then back again, enhanced somehow. She nestled closer. He felt good, firmer than a pillow or teddy bear for sure but still cuddly somehow.

Closing her eyes, she forced down her worry and managed to drift off to sleep.

***

Juliet's eyes fluttered open to find bright light seeping around the cracks of the door. Back to daytime lighting? Something heavy rested across her. She craned her neck. Sandstorm's arm was draped over her side, his hand pressed against her waist, pulling her into his body. She traced her hand up his arm and onto his neck. His pulse beat steadily, and he felt warm but not feverishly so. Relief coursed through her, and she lay still, just savoring the fact that he had made it through the night.

Sometime during the night, they'd shifted a lot. She vaguely remembered some of it. The mild half-awake shock of waking up when her "pillow" moved, followed by a split second of reorienting herself, remembering he was in bed with her and why, then settling down and getting cozy again.

Man, my parents would have a fit if they saw me getting spooned by a supervillain.

She laughed quietly and touched his wrist. His hand was still clenched around something, she assumed that bottle cap. That had to be some strong memory. She'd interrogate him about that later.

After a few minutes of lying still, enjoying the silence, her stomach rumbled. Were they ever going to feed her? Or check on him? Sure, Diamondback wanted them both dead, but Wallace and Mentallica had always seemed reasonable.

She managed to extricate herself from under his arm and slip from the bed. After taking a moment to pull the blanket back over him, she retreated to the bathroom to do her best to freshen up. Her hair looked frazzled, so she french braided it. It came out okay. Maybe slightly lopsided, but who was she trying to impress anyway?

She'd just finished brushing her teeth when she heard a muffled voice from the bedroom.

Her breath caught in her chest. Was he up?

She hurried to his side to find his blurry eyes fluttering open.

He was finally conscious. That had to be a good sign, right?

"Hey you." She dabbed at his forehead with her sleeve. "How are you feeling?"

"Mushy—" he muttered, his eyes falling shut again.

She tilted her head to one side. "Mushy?"

Once more, his eyes opened, this time meeting hers. "You changed your hair."

"Uh, yeah." She touched the braids.

He gave a dopey smile. "You're cute."

"Okay—" she drew out the word.

"Just itty-bitty. Sometimes I want to put you in my pocket and carry you around—like a ferret." He practically giggled. "Itty-bitty pocket ferret—"

"Man, that venom must be strong stuff." She clicked her tongue. "Do you think you could drink some water?"

He nodded but immediately hid his face in the pillow and fell silent.

So doing better but not all there yet.

Juliet waited a moment, but when his eyes remained closed and his breath steadied, she gave up and returned to the bathroom to wash her face.

Someone rapped on the door. She froze. Not Diamondback. He wouldn't knock.

"Who is it?" she called out.

"Mentallica. I'm coming in anyway. That was just a warning."

Juliet exited the bathroom as Mentallica entered. She held two plates of eggs, toast, and bacon. The smell of the bacon—after days of bland sandwiches, plain oatmeal, and fake eggs—caused Juliet's mouth to immediately water.

Mentallica glanced towards the bed. "I didn't know if ... is he okay?"

"He's alive," Juliet said. "Still delirious, but his fever's gone and he doesn't seem to be in pain."

"He probably isn't ready to eat this then. Maybe you'll want both of them. I'm not hungry." Mentallica passed her the two paper plates. Juliet placed them on the bedside table before facing Mentallica again.

"Thank you."

Instead of leaving, Mentallica continued to stare past Juliet towards Sandstorm. "Diamondback better pray Lucas gets through this. If he doesn't ... well, let's just say, he'll need to watch his back from now on."

Juliet bit her bottom lip. "You care about him, don't you?"

Mentallica's mouth twitched. "We're villains. We don't care."

"Sorry, I didn't realize villain was code for robot."

Juliet rolled her eyes.

Mentallica's lips curled into what might have been the start of a smile, but then her expression hardened. She continued to focus on Sandstorm. "Black Fox loyalty only goes one way. They expect total from you, but they'll only really look out for you if they need you. In this game, your function matters more than anything else. If what you bring to the team isn't worth the cost of keeping you around, then they won't. Sandstorm isn't like that. A few years ago, before we brought Diamondback on, it was me and him, Wallace, and a heat-manipulating sable called Lucifer. Lucifer was our team's heavy hitter, but a literal and figurative hothead. One time we were raiding a DOSA weapons stash, and he ... well, all I remember was one minute I was accessing the computer manifests when there was a big boom and then suddenly everything was on fire." She pulled up the hem of her T-shirt revealing a series of burn scars across her stomach and side. "Wallace called an immediate abort. I *think* Lucifer died in the initial blast. At least I never saw him again. She ordered Sandstorm, who was on the perimeter, to retreat. He ignored her and came in after me. Nearly killed himself. Even fragmented he needs to breathe and can burn. So care for him? No. Realize that you don't get a teammate who will put your life above orders all that often in this business? Yes."

Juliet nodded slowly. "He ... how did he even end up here? He doesn't seem like he fits into the life."

"The story is he almost got out." Mentallica shrugged. "He doesn't talk about it, but villains gossip like old women, especially in a gang like this. He left for a few years a while back, before the Sand Foxes and the Blackwood Syndicate merged to create our supposed 'super' gang." She scoffed. "Really super now. We're all that remains of it. It's like we're destined to eat ourselves up from the inside."

"He got out?" Juliet prodded. Maybe it was weird, but

she needed to understand who he was. The contradiction of him was driving her crazy.

"Yeah, disappeared so completely the gang had him as 'dead' in their records. Then his uncle, Vic Lucas, the Sand Fox chief, found him and somehow dragged him in for one more job. Bank heist. Supposed to be cut and dried, but a security guard was killed—while restrained to make it even worse. After that, Sandstorm ended up on DOSA's most wanted list. Like I said, he won't talk about it, but I'm pretty sure it was his uncle, not Lucas himself, who killed the guard. DOSA is kind of picky about the felony murder thing, though, and they're not going to cut him slack just because he wasn't the trigger man."

Juliet swallowed. That made a little more sense than imagining Sandstorm as a complete villain. Didn't excuse his current status, but she could believe it more.

"Don't be an idiot," Mentallica said, interrupting her thoughts.

Juliet started. "What?"

"Look, DOSA girl, I know your name's Juliet, but that doesn't give you an excuse to try to drag my teammate into a tragic romance." Mentallica scowled.

Juliet's jaw clenched. "I'm not—"

"Yeah, you are. I see it, and you know what will happen if he falls for you? He'll get killed. Probably you too, but I don't care as much about that."

Juliet's face heated, but she returned Mentallica's scowl. "I thought you didn't care at all?"

"Whatever. Just don't be stupid." Mentallica stormed out of the room.

Juliet let out a long breath before going to pick up one of the plates of food. In spite of her previous appetite, she couldn't bring herself to take a bite. She put the food back down and sat on the edge of the bed next to Sandstorm, allowing herself to stroke his hair once more.

I'm not falling for him. I'm not. I can't ... it's all part of the plan, get him to trust me, to like me even, then ...

escape.

Even as she tried to believe it, though, she could remember the warm indulgence of lying next to him the night before, the cold fear that pierced her heart when Diamondback attacked him, the goofy grin on his face when he idiotically called her a "cute pocket ferret."

Why did he have to be a supervillain?

Chapter Thirteen

Juliet forced herself to eat her breakfast. After a few bites, her appetite reawakened, and she devoured both portions of eggs and one strip of bacon. The toast and remaining bacon she set aside in case he wanted them when he woke up. Cold eggs were gross, but cold bacon and toast would be mostly edible, after all.

She checked on Sandstorm again. Still sleeping. That had to be a good sign, right?

She knelt beside the bed and examined his face. "Come on, Sandy. You can get through this."

He'd shifted again, to lie on his side this time, his eyes closed, his lips just barely parted. A sudden desire to kiss him welled up within her. In a fairy tale, that would wake someone up. Not that she thought it would work but ... it couldn't hurt, could it?

Is that a consent issue, though? I mean, it's just a kiss—but if he kissed me while I was sleeping, I'd probably want to punch him. Yeah, better not.

She rested the back of her hand against his cheek and forehead, pretending to check his temperature even though he hadn't had a fever in hours.

Her mind churned. This was so stupid. She knew who he was, what he was—but did she really? Mentallica's story made sense, but other details didn't fit. Like why was he protecting her? What did he mean about staying on the path, even if he was delirious?

Instead of withdrawing her hand, she brushed her fingers back up into his hair. As she did, his eyes fluttered open.

Her throat tightened. "How do you feel?"

"My head hurts," he said.

"Here." She picked the first aid kit off the floor and found the packet of Advil. Tearing this open she squeezed out the two pills from within. "Take these."

He opened his hand and held it out to her. The bottle cap still rested in his palm. He managed to pop the pills into his mouth before tucking the cap somewhere under the blanket, probably in his jean pocket.

"How long was I out?"

"Overnight ... plus a few more hours. It's hard to mark time in here," she said. "Hopefully that medicine works. What's the last thing you remember?"

"Lying down here." He rested his forehead in his hand. "I mean, there's a few other things after that, but they're pretty blurry and some of them don't make sense. Hallucinations and dreams, maybe?"

"You were talking in your sleep a couple of times." She nodded.

"That doesn't surprise me. Where's my jacket and shoes?"

"I'll get them." She returned his belongings to him.

"Thanks." Sandstorm sat up but immediately slumped over, holding his head in his hands. "Ouch."

"Are you okay?" Juliet rested her hand on his upper back.

"Getting there." He drew several deep breaths. "Do you have any water? My mouth feels like I've been sucking on cotton balls."

"Yeah, just a second." She entered the tiny bathroom and filled up the empty water bottle before bringing it back to him. He sipped slowly.

"Thanks for staying with me through that," he then said. "I don't remember much after getting dosed, but from how I feel right now and how hazy everything is—it was rough."

"Yeah, it was." She sat beside him on the mattress. Her hand almost returned to his back, but instead she folded her hands in her lap, watching him as he put his shoes and jacket back on. "Can I ask you a question?"

"Shoot." He took a longer swig, emptying the bottle, then set it aside.

"You said you didn't have parents," she said.

"Nope. I sprang fully formed out of the ground." His eyes twinkled, a sign that he was truly on the mend, she supposed, but still irritating.

"Don't be flippant," she chided.

"I only have a sixth-grade education. You're gonna need to use smaller words." He ran his fingers back through his sandy brown hair, pushing it away from his eyes and forehead.

She narrowed her eyes at him. He sighed.

"Okay, everyone has parents. I just never knew mine. They were both dead by the time I was two. Why?"

"Because you called out to your mom when you were hallucinating. Several times."

His face reddened. "That's ... embarrassing. Did ... what else did I say?"

"Something about staying on the path. The rest was mostly whimpering." Yeah, a little cruel, but man, the guy was frustrating.

"Huh." He focused on his feet. "I guess maybe my subconscious remembers being two better than I do." He tried to stand but wobbled and sat heavily beside her again, his face going gray.

"Stay down, you idiot!" She took the empty bottle from him. "I'll get you some more."

As she refilled the bottle, she glanced over her shoulder at him. His head stayed down, his shoulders rising and falling in great breaths. Her heart twisted. He'd almost died, and for what? To protect her. He wouldn't be fighting with his teammates if it wasn't for her. Before her captivity things had been so black and white, DOSA vs. villains, her vs. them, but now ... if Sandstorm died because of her, she'd hate it.

It can't last. They have no plans to let me go, and it'll

only get harder for him to convince them not to kill me. Eventually he'll have to choose between keeping me safe and keeping his peace with them, and it's not like villain gangs just let people quit. They'll kill him ... or they'll kill me ... or both of us. It's the only way this ends.

Cold water ran over her hand as the bottle overflowed. She quickly shut off the tap, switched the dripping bottle into her other hand, and shook the droplets off her fingers.

If I escape, that's ideal for me, but if I do ... they'll blame him if he's close to me. Asking him for help is as good as asking him to die for me, and ... oh gosh ...

She kicked herself. There were people out there in danger because of the Black Foxes' plan. Innocent people —and she was worried about a supervillain? Was she starting to get Stockholm Syndrome or something? All the more reason to get out of here.

She returned to his side and offered him the water bottle.

"Thanks," he said, straightening again. Some color had returned to his cheeks though his eyes were bloodshot.

"Eating might make you feel better. Do you think you could keep some food down?" she asked.

"Maybe, but I'm fine. I just stood up too fast." He took another drink then set the bottle to the side. "Juliet—it's going to get harder and harder to keep them from hurting you. If Wallace didn't stop Diamondback from attacking me, she's not going to say anything about him attacking you, and—well—" He avoided her eyes. "I have to think of a new plan."

She stared at him, wishing she had Mentallica's powers. "Why are you ... why do you care what happens to me? You're going along with a plan that could hurt so many people. Why am I more important than any of them?"

He hung his head. "I do what I can to stop things

from getting out of hand. If everything goes right, no one will get hurt."

"And if they do?" she asked.

He shrugged. "That's the business. I never claimed to be anything but a villain. What did you expect?"

Her insides twisted. "Okay, but then ... why me?"

He looked up, meeting her gaze, and a shiver cut through her. "I don't know those people. They aren't my responsibility. You? I brought you here, got you into this mess, and I promised myself I wouldn't let you die because of it. Maybe I'm a villain, but when I make a promise, I keep it. That's all you need to know."

Irritation flared within her. "That doesn't make any sense. You don't ..."

"Look, do you want me to tell Diamondback he can have at you?" he snapped. "Is that what you want? For me to be *consistent*, step out of the way, and let my gang chew you up and spit you out? Because you know, princess, that would be a lot easier for me."

She quailed back, realizing how close she was coming to alienating her one remaining ally.

His mouth pinched. "Things aren't as simple as your little good guys, bad guys game of cops and robbers you play with DOSA. They never have been, and I don't have the luxury of being all one thing. I'm a villain, but I'm still human enough not to want to see you hurt, and that's all you need to know—"

He tried to stand, but she grabbed his arm. "Wait—"

He stood anyway, pulling her along for the ride. She gasped and stumbled, falling against his chest. He caught her, staring down at her. Her tongue stuck to the roof of her mouth as she stood—or leaned—with one hand pressed against his taut chest, the other still clutching his bicep. She could feel his warmth through his T-shirt, the rise and fall of his breath. Their eyes met, his hazel with flecks of green. Her breath abandoned her. His lower lip went slack, and against her better judgment, she gave into her instincts, her hand slipping up his chest onto his neck. He drew closer, encircling her, his hands easing onto her back. For a moment she could feel his breath against her cheek, but at the last moment, he turned away, closing his eyes, his arms still around her, but his face angled from hers.

"This is a bad idea," he whispered.

"I'm all out of good ones," she said with a quavering laugh.

He released her, putting both hands on her shoulders for a moment to steady her, then stepped back. His eyes swept over her, a hunger within them that mirrored her own, before he turned away and took a step towards the door.

"Don't go!" The words slipped from her before she could stop them. He paused, and humiliation flooded through her. What did she even want out of this? It wasn't like it could go anywhere productive. "Never mind." She fell back a step and hugged herself, desperately trying to process what had almost happened. Her lips still tingled from the near miss, and his warmth played about her, especially where his hands had grasped her arms. A primal admiration for the strength of his hold, for the way he towered over her but moved with such control and gentleness, sparked within her like a fire. She kicked herself for not making the final move to get that kiss. After all, if she was likely to die soon anyway, what did she have to lose?

Sandstorm cleared his throat and put his hand on the door. "I need to check in with my team. See if I can patch things up with Wallace—"

"Wallace was willing to leave you for dead, Sandy," she protested. "You don't owe her anything."

He didn't look at her. "That's the game. The beef between me and Huxley isn't her problem. It's our job to sort it out, and if that involves one of us biting it—"

"This is ridiculous." She grabbed his shoulder, pulling

him to face her. "You don't belong with them."

"I kinda do," he said.

"You're not like them, though!" Was she really doing this? She'd fought the suspicion that there was more to him than the others, that he was better somehow. It had to be wishful thinking fueled by his easy smile and sparkling eyes and ... oh man, that mouth. She bit her bottom lip hard to stop herself from thinking about that. "There's something off about them. Wallace is heartless. Mentallica is bitter. Diamondback is ... a complete waste of breath. Their insides are messed up and it exudes from everything they do and say. You, you're ... you're still whole somehow." She reached up and rested her hand on his cheek. He didn't pull away though his mouth twisted as if he were tasting something bitter. "There's something strong and straight and right in you, Sandstorm or Lucas or whatever your name is. I can feel it. I can see it in the way you've treated me when everyone else here—" Her voice cracked. "You don't have to put up with this. We could leave—together."

"You do remember I'm a villain, right?" he murmured. "I've done things. Yeah, I'm not far gone enough to want to see you killed, but that doesn't make me a good person."

"There's hope. There's ... there's the Supervillain Rehabilitation Project." How had she forgotten that? Her own sister-in-law had been a subject, pulled out of a life of villainy to become a DOSA hero. If that could happen for Katie, it could happen for Sandstorm.

The corner of his mouth twitched. "Supervillain Rehabilitation Project, huh?"

"DOSA's been running it for years. They've turned dozens of villains around and made them heroes. You could do it." Her hold on him tightened. "I know you could."

His shoulders slumped. "Juliet—I ... It's not that simple. I have a job to do, and I'm going to do it, but ..."

His mouth shut. He trailed his fingers across her cheek and into her hair for a moment, his eyes so intent upon her face that her insides quivered like a puppy praying to be scooped up and cuddled. "Whatever happens, I won't let you be hurt. I have one sliver of my soul left, and if they hurt you, I'll lose it. I'm not going to let that happen. I promise." He plucked her hand from his shoulder and slipped out of her grasp, fragmenting through the doorway before she could say another word.

Her knees buckled. What the heck had she gotten herself into?

Chapter Fourteen

Sandstorm sat in the break room with a steaming bowl of packaged ramen noodles. Diamondback and Mentallica's restock had gone without a hitch. The kitchen cabinets and fridge were full again. Wanting to get something in his stomach fast, he'd made the quickest and easiest thing he could think of.

His head still hurt, and his stomach felt like he'd been riding a roller coaster for hours. He needed to get his strength back before something else happened, and with everything hurtling towards chaos, something else was bound to happen soon.

Footsteps sounded in the hallway, and he sat up straighter, staring at the door. His powers flickered through him, ready in case it was Diamondback and the jerk wanted to throw down again. Instead, Mentallica entered. Surprise crossed her face.

"You're up?"

"Apparently." He spooned up a little bit of broth, blew on it, and slurped it down.

"I checked in on you this morning," she said. "You were still pretty out of it."

"I don't feel too hot right now either, but I'm getting there." He continued to eat. "Where are Diamondback and Wallace?"

"Diamondback hasn't left his room since your tiff." She sat across the break room table from him. "Sulking because Wallace chewed him out. Wallace and I have been working on the last few steps for the mission."

Sandstorm's stomach twisted, and he slowed his pace with the soup. "We're getting close?"

"If I can binge the last bit of coding without any

distractions, then, yeah, I can have it ready by tomorrow," she said. "I told Wallace, and she asked why we're keeping the prisoner then, if we're so close. I told her you were working on something, but are you? We haven't even put the screws to Surge yet. That was the whole point of her captivity."

Sandstorm reached into his pocket for his bottle cap. "I've spent so much time dealing with Diamondback's crap, I haven't had a chance to work on the Surge plan. If we're about to put things into action, though, he might be more useful than ever. We'll want a direct line into DOSA HQ when the mission is going down."

"True. Do you think he'll come through with it? I mean, I know she's his sister, but she's just one life, and our plan is putting thousands in the line of fire. Hundreds of thousands." She leaned across the table. "When he's got to choose, surely the numbers—"

"That's not how family works," Sandstorm interrupted.

"And what do you know about family?" She sniffed.

"Let's just say I got the prisoner to open up about their relationship, and they're close. He'll do what it takes to keep her alive," Sandstorm said.

"Is that all she 'opened up' to you about?" Mentallica arched her eyebrows.

Sandstorm winced. "You've been listening to Diamondback."

"No. I've just noticed you spend a lot of time with the little DOSA princess." She crossed her arms over her chest. "Even got all cozy with her while you were injured."

"She kept me alive, but I've been keeping her alive, so we're even." He took a large bite of noodles and loudly sucked them out of the bowl, hoping she'd go away.

She gagged. "Stop being a brat. I'm just trying to figure out if I need to be worried about you."

"You don't." He focused on his meal, trying to ignore the prickling feeling in his head.

Get out of my brain. There's nothing to see here.

So if Wallace orders you to get rid of the girl, it won't be an issue?

Sandstorm couldn't stop the shudder of revulsion and dread that rippled through him.

"Yeah, you're not okay," she said.

He focused on her. "You've never had to kill anyone, have you?"

She shrugged. "It's never come up. Not my power set."

"Yeah, well as someone who has, trust me, it's not like robbing a convenience store or planning a bank heist. It's … I just hope you never have to learn." Appetite completely gone, he pushed aside his bowl. "So yeah, I don't want to be responsible for ending Juliet Park's life, but if we're smart, I won't have to. I'm fine. Worry about doing your job, and I'll keep being that way."

"If you say so." Her eyes clouded. "I guess we're all complicit in that test run bombing, though. Not sure what my percentage of the blame is there. It feels distant and unreal, you know? It's kinda lucky the timer malfunctioned. If it had gone off during business hours like Wallace intended, there would've been a lot more people in the building. Almost like someone intended it that way." She eyed him pointedly, and Sandstorm made a point of tracing the noodles in his bowl rather than thinking about the bombing. After a moment the scratching in his head died down, and he relaxed slightly.

"It was still six deaths. I wouldn't call that lucky." Sandstorm dumped the remainder of his ramen down the garbage disposal. He'd tried to talk Wallace out of that "show of power." His influence over her was unpredictable at best. Sometimes he swore she stopped listening to him arbitrarily to prove to the others that she was in control of the team, not him. "Look, I'm going to put a few things in place regarding Surge. Did you set it up so I can reach him through the Burnr app without

DOSA catching on?"

"You should be good." She nodded.

"Thanks. I might have an idea of how we can use him, but it's a work in progress." He rubbed the back of his neck. "Can you keep an eye on Diamondback for me? He's not going to be happy to hear I survived. Might do something stupid."

"I'll try, but Wallace is going to want me to finish up the code."

Great. Now he had to babysit Diamondback as well as do his job.

"Do what you can. I'll check in shortly. I need a shower." He strode out of the kitchen towards the locker room where the spare showers were. He needed a plan. Time was running out.

Chapter Fifteen

Juliet knelt beside her bed, working on the screws that held the board at the end of it with Sandstorm's multi-tool. A board wasn't the best weapon, but it would be more likely to go unnoticed beside the door than the knife or the lid to the toilet tank.

She'd just unfastened the second screw when the creaking of the deadbolt alerted her to someone entering. Without much time, she dropped the multi-tool, kicked it under the bed, and spun around. Hopefully whoever it was wouldn't notice the missing screws.

Her insides clenched when Diamondback entered, shutting the door behind him. Maybe she should've kept the multi-tool. She could use something to stab with right about now.

"What do you want?"

"Just to give you a warning." Diamondback leaned against the door. He leered at her, and she shifted uncomfortably, even though she was wearing the baggiest pair of sweatpants and sweatshirt possible—both belonging to Mentallica who was several inches taller than her and broader at the hips and shoulders.

"A warning?" she repeated.

He nodded. "You should choose your allies carefully, sweetheart. We're all here at Wallace's leisure and sucking up to Lucas will only get you so far. If you want to survive this, you'll need to be on all of our good sides."

She wrinkled her nose. "I don't think you have a good side. Besides, I've seen you interact with Wallace. If you step out of line again, she'll kick you back down. You've already lost a chunk of your share. Do you really want to risk losing more?"

She hoped that wasn't a bluff.

"You really think that Sand Rat is going to be your savior?" Diamondback sneered. "He's a Lucas. They're all garbage."

"And you have so many stones to throw." She eyed the door behind him. He hadn't locked it, but the chances of getting by him were pretty slim. She could maybe depend on being faster, but fast enough to make it to the portal disks and escape? Probably not.

"He's not what you think. He pretends to be above it all, but he's as dirty as any one of us." His eyes glinted.

"Say what you want, but at least he's keeping me alive and safe." She crossed her arms over her chest.

"Only because he's using you, sweetheart," Diamondback said.

"Whatever." She stuck her chin in the air. "Think what you want. He hasn't laid a hand on me like that."

Realization crept across his face. "You don't know? No, of course, you wouldn't. It's not like he'd risk his shiny exterior to tell you."

"Tell me what?" she asked.

"The con he's running on your heroic big brother?"

Juliet stiffened. "What are you talking about?"

"Why do you think he's keeping you alive? Villains don't do anything for free. Me? I would've been happy to let you stay breathing for a few simple—favors." He eyed her again, and bile tainted her mouth. "Lucas, though? He's more strategic. He's running a long game, using your life as leverage to get DOSA's hot shot, Surge, to feed us intel."

The blood drained from her face. "Shawn wouldn't—"

"To stop you from getting killed? Yeah, he would. It surprised me too, but not Lucas. He knows people. How to use them. How to get them to do what he wants, even Wallace. Definitely you."

Her hands shook. It couldn't be true. "You're lying. I have no reason to trust you—"

"Like you said to me, think what you want—" The door burst open behind him, knocking into his back. He stumbled forward as Sandstorm entered, glaring at him.

"What are you doing in here?" he asked. "Haven't you learned yet—"

Diamondback steadied himself, turned to face Sandstorm, and held up his hands. "I was just leaving. You and your girlfriend have a lot to talk about." He walked right through Sandstorm's fragmented form. As Sandstorm's particles reformed in Diamondback's wake, his brow furrowed.

Diamondback left, shutting the door behind them and locking the deadbolt for good measure.

Sandstorm stepped closer to her, putting out his hand to touch her face. "Are you okay? He didn't—"

"Stop!" She pulled away.

His hand fell to his side, his eyes widening.

"Is it true what he said? About ... about Shawn?"

His Adam's apple bobbed. "Jules—"

"No, you don't get to call me that," she growled.

He shut his mouth.

She searched his face, begging for a sign that he didn't know what she was talking about, that it was all a cruel trick. Nothing presented.

Juliet's insides quivered with a mix of disgust and horror.

"Is it true?" she repeated. "Are you blackmailing my brother?"

Sandstorm's expression remained inscrutable though his eyes lost their usual glimmer, becoming stony.

"What do you want me to say? Did you think we were keeping you alive for the fun of it? Just to have around? We're villains. We don't do anything if it doesn't benefit us or our plans. Yeah, I'm using you to get to your brother, but it's the only reason you're alive."

Her heart faltered. What would happen to Shawn? He'd never betray DOSA. It wasn't who he was, but he also wouldn't allow her to come to harm. That also wasn't who he was. This had to be tearing him apart.

And I've sat here letting it happen. Trusting the one who is doing it to him. I thought I was playing Sandstorm, but he was playing me. I'm such an idiot.

Humiliation welled within her only to immediately boil into rage.

"You ... Shawn is the best man I know, the best person I know. He's kind and ethical. He's everything I should be but I'm not! The two things that matter the most to him are his honor as a hero and his family, and you're making him choose between them!"

Sandstorm didn't flinch.

"You're a monster! How could you pretend to ... I thought you were different, human at least, but it was all a lie. You're worse than all of them." She shoved him towards the door. For once he didn't use his powers, her hands impacting against his chest, but not budging him. "I'd rather die than hurt Shawn like that. If that's all that's keeping me alive, fine. Kill me. Don't hide behind your supposed last remnants of a soul. That sliver you said was left? It's a lie. It's gone. There's nothing in you worth caring about, nothing worth saving, and I'd rather die by your hand than live one more moment under your protection." She shoved him again, harder this time.

His mouth opened, then closed, then he nodded. His body shimmered, and he fragmented through the door.

Frustration exploded within her. He wasn't even going to fight her?

"I hope you rot!" she screamed at the door. "I hope you rot and burn and die and ... oh ..." She collapsed to her knees, weeping.

She'd been a fool, and Shawn was paying the price. She'd hesitated too long. She needed to get out of here. She needed to get out of here now. Sniffing back tears, she returned to the bed and fished out the multi-tool.

Tonight she was going to escape or die trying.

***

Sandstorm didn't return to his solid form until he'd made the elevator and the closing doors blocked out her shouts. Once there he leaned against the wall and slid down to the floor, his knees against his chest and his face in his hands.

How else did you think this was going to end? You made choices. Yes, they kept her alive, but you knew there would be consequences. Did you expect her to accept you torturing her brother?

He desperately sought the bottle cap in his pocket. He squeezed it in his fist until it cut into his hand.

I just need to get through. I just need to find the other side. I've given up so much. I can't stop now. I can't. Even if ... even if it feels like death.

This was the farthest he'd been from the path since this whole mess started. Maybe she was right. Maybe there was no coming back from this one. Maybe his compromise to keep her safe had cost him his last sliver of soul, but if so it was worth it as long as he could keep her alive through to the end.

A few more days. Dear God, let me get through it.

If Juliet was no longer going to accept his help, he had less time than he'd hoped. This was a risk, but he needed to take it. Pausing and clearing his head, he tried to discern any sense of Mentallica reading him. Nothing. Good sign, but he still needed to be quick.

He fished his phone out of his pocket. With no one outside of his gang to call, he rarely carried it with him around the lair, but he'd been psyching himself up for the last hour to contact Surge. Now he needed to do so fast.

He accessed the Burnr app. While supposedly the app deleted all messages permanently after they were read, with Mentallica's skill set, he couldn't be sure of this. Was he willing to bet everything?

Yeah, for her, I am.

Selecting Surge's contact information he tapped out a

message.

Your sister is running out of time. You need to contact Talon. Tell him the truth. Tell him everything. Tell him Lucia's kid is calling in a favor. He'll give you what you need.

He intentionally focused on counting ceiling titles, all the while scanning for any sign of Mentallica.

A reply popped up. **Who is this?**

Sandstorm immediately deleted the conversation. That was done. For the rest, he needed to move fast.

***

Shawn stared at the phone. He started to type out another response only to have the whole conversation blink out followed by a "chat not found" error message.

What the heck is going on?

He stood up from the break room chair where he'd been sulking, not really doing anything or thinking anything but simmering about how few options he had.

It wasn't near any meal times so the break room was empty, but still too public. He hurried down the hallway, mulling over the strange message.

I'm a nobody. Well, a DOSA hero in good standing, but not anyone committee chief Talon would take a call from. The guy practically runs DOSA. To get to him, I'll have to jump through so many hoops and middlemen—and for what? So I can tell him I've been compromised and my sister will die if I don't betray the agency he's made his life's work? There's no way. He'll have me arrested and Juliet ... this has to be a trap? Or a test? But to what end?

He rode the elevator up, managing to avoid any other agents. Finally alone in his room, he fiddled with the Burnr app, trying to find the contact who had messaged him. Burnr app IDs were random strings of characters, and while he could remember a few, it didn't match any of his current contacts. It had to be the supervillains who had Juliet, but why would they be telling him to confess to the DOSA chief?

Shawn's stomach twisted. He was out of time and options and things were only getting worse.

This is impossible. If I call up DC HQ, there's no way Talon will take my call—but—

Breathing a prayer, Shawn dialed his father.

Dave Park answered almost immediately. "Shawn, hello. Any news?"

Shawn exhaled. "No, but Dad, I need a big favor from you, but I can't explain why. Will you trust me?"

"Yes," his dad said firmly. "What is it?"

"I need to talk to Talon."

There was a moment of silence then Dave gave a low whistle. "You weren't lying about the 'big' part of the favor."

"Do you have his number?" Shawn said.

"Yes. Got it a few years ago after I closed an important case, but the specifications were emergencies only. I'm assuming this applies?"

"It does." Maybe Shawn had a chance to get through this. His phone buzzed. He checked his notifications and found his father had sent him a contact card.

"It's his personal line. I've never had to use it, but my understanding is he always picks up."

"Thanks, Dad. I owe you one." Without waiting for a response, Shawn disconnected the call and dialed Talon.

"Who is this?" a deep voice with a slight southern drawl answered after two rings.

"Shawn Park, AKA Surge, hero with the Columbus team, sir."

"How'd you get this number, son?"

"My dad."

"Park—? Ah, you're Verve's boy. Good man, your father. You have thirty seconds."

Shawn considered his words carefully. "Do the words 'Lucia's kid' mean anything to you?"

Talon drew in a hissing breath. "That ... what do you

need?"

"It's a long story. Are we still on the thirty-second limit?"

"No. Fill me in."

"Well, sir, are you aware of what's going on with my sister in Pittsburgh?"

Chapter Sixteen

Juliet tucked the steak knife into a thigh sheath she'd made out of snake-bite bandages and a torn-up blanket. She pulled her longest top, a hoodie Mentallica had loaned her that seemed to be a men's extra large for some reason, over it. This done, she leaned the board she'd dismantled from the foot of the bed beside the door.

That was two weapons. Wouldn't do her much good if she couldn't catch her captor's unaware, though. After all, they had superpowers, and currently, she didn't. What she really needed was the remote control for her disruptor cuff.

She checked her pocket for the zip ties and pulled the pillowcase off the pillow and stuck that in the front pocket of her hoodie too. She still had Sandstorm's multi-tool. Maybe she could get the hinges off the door again. That had worked once.

Once I get out of this room, I won't have a lot of time. I should go straight for the drawer with the teleportation disks, but I have to get information on where they've planted the bombs first. I know those are on the computer. If I can get a peek at them, I can memorize the locations, maybe. Though a printout or some sort of way to transfer the information would be better.

She approached the door. Should probably wait until the nighttime lighting kicked on. It wasn't a sure thing, but the villains did seem to keep a fairly regular sleep schedule.

Footsteps approached, and she moved back into the center of the room, listening. The door opened, and Mentallica entered, carrying a plate with what appeared to be boxed mac and cheese on it. Seeing the mind reader, Juliet's brain short-circuited, jumping through so many things she didn't want her to read her mind about.

Quick, what did Sandstorm say? Focus on anything else.

She locked onto the first safe thing that popped into her mind, her mother's actual mac and cheese recipe. The one with bacon and crunchy breadcrumbs on top. Having grown up in Korea, American comfort food wasn't necessarily Ara Park's specialty, but when her daughter had gone to a birthday party and come home raving about this wonderful new dish, mac and cheese that tasted so much better than the boxed stuff, she'd determined to learn it. Eventually Mom had perfected the recipe and usually made it on Juliet's birthday. Juliet adored it even when it started giving her digestive issues. Her mom's mac and cheese had been worth some stomach cramps. This stuff, probably not.

"Sorry, this doesn't have bacon in it." Mentallica passed the plate to Juliet.

So you are reading my mind. Juliet hoped her irritation came through with the thought.

Mentallica looked around the room. "Diamondback's been bragging about how he broke you and Sandstorm up. What's the about?"

"He told me about my brother." The rage rose within Juliet again, giving her another good focus point.

"That'd do it. Well, it had to happen, though I hated seeing Diamondback so smug. Of course, Sandstorm's plan actually working deflated him again." Mentallica chuckled. "That brother of yours came through. Sent a huge file of classified DOSA documents to the digital dropbox I set up for him. It's going to take me a few days to go through it all and see what we can do with it, but it's well worth keeping you around for that."

Juliet's heart sank. *Oh, Shawn, no.*

"Hey, don't look so glum, DOSA girl," Mentallica said. "It means your brother loves you, after all."

"Go to hell," Juliet shot back. "And take Sandstorm with you."

"Awful feisty for a girl in a cage." Mentallica shoved the paper plate into Juliet's hands. "It's molten hot. Maybe a little burned too, but you can't really tell with this stuff. Enjoy, I guess."

She turned around, exposing her back to Juliet.

Acting instinctively so that Mentallica wouldn't have time to read her thoughts, Juliet lunged forward and dumped the steaming mac and cheese down Mentallica's shirt. The villainess shrieked.

"You little—" She flailed her arms, trying to wipe away the sticky, hot mess off the back of her neck. Juliet sprang, grabbed Mentallica by both wrists, and yanked her arms down. She drove her knee up into Mentallica's kidney. Mentallica cried out in pain and crumpled to her knees.

Wanting to avoid Mentallica's sleep-touch trick, Juliet acted fast. She whipped out her zip ties, secured Mentallica's wrists behind her back, and shoved the pillowcase over her head for good measure.

Mentallica managed to get enough breath out to give a muffled yelp, but Juliet didn't stop. She pushed her away and ran out of the room, slamming and deadbolting the door behind her.

Okay, no going back now. Computers?

It was a risk, but if she didn't discover the locations of the bombs, her captivity—and Shawn's betrayal of DOSA —would be for nothing. It was her one chance to redeem them both, herself for her stupidity and him for his compassion. She climbed the ladder to the next level and paused to listen. No screaming or shouting. How much time did she have, though?

She slipped into the hall and hugged the wall, headed towards the computer room. Security cameras watched her from multiple angles, but from what she'd seen exploring the lair with Sandstorm, no one was actively watching the feeds. Hopefully by the time someone checked back the tapes, she'd be long gone.

As she reached the door to the command center, a sound caught her ears: the clicking of keyboard keys.

Her heart sank. Someone was in the room, working. The door was slightly ajar. She crept by it and peered in.

Sandstorm bent over the keyboard, standing rather than sitting. He tapped a few more keys then pulled what appeared to be a thumb drive out of the computer tower. Juliet shied back. Without her powers, she couldn't face him. She passed the door and hurried to the port-in room, shutting herself in it and locking the door behind her. That might buy her a little time to figure things out.

This is one time I can't be a hero. If I don't get out of here, they'll keep using Shawn. Even if I don't know the locations, I can at least tell them about the bombs. If I had my powers back, though—then I might have a chance to do both.

She went first for the portal drawer, unlocked it with the code she'd watched Sandstorm use, and then took a disk out. She stuck it in her hoodie's thankfully large front pocket before deciding that it might be good to have a backup and grabbing another to go along with it.

This achieved, she started to open other drawers. The first two yielded nothing of use, be the third...

Jackpot.

She grinned down at the collection of both disruptor cuffs and remotes. She pocketed two disruptor cuffs, just in case, then took one of the remotes.

"Going somewhere?" a sardonic voice asked.

She whirled around and found Sandstorm leaning against the door, watching her.

For a half-second she gaped at him. She'd locked the door. How ... oh. Dang him.

"Nowhere you need to bother your little head about." She pushed the button. The disruptor on her ankle whirred and hit the floor. Her power surged through her like fresh air through her lungs after ages of holding her breath. "How'd you know I was in here?"

He nodded to the security camera. "Had a feeling. Checked the feeds. You know I can't just let you go. If Wallace watches the playback and sees you walked out without a fight, she'll kill me."

"I'd be broken up about that." She rolled her eyes.

"Yeah, I figured you wouldn't count that as a con, but I thought I'd mention it." He lazily peeled himself off the wall. "So how do you want to do this?"

"Like this!" She threw her hands forward, channeling as much willpower as she could into an energy blast.

Sandstorm fragmented around her blast like dirt particles fleeing a drop of dish soap. He coalesced into his human form again but still shimmered.

"This could take a while." He winked at her.

Something within Juliet snapped, and she charged forward, swinging one of the disruptor cuffs like a whip, hoping to catch him with it and thwart his abilities. Sandstorm broke apart. She rushed through him, and he solidified behind her. His hand clamped down on her shoulder.

"Missed me."

Her fist clipped through his face. He fell back, even though she hadn't made any solid contact. Her heart raced. Maybe he couldn't beat her, but she couldn't lay a hand on him, and all he needed to do was stall her until his teammates found them. She couldn't take on the whole gang.

Think, Juliet. Think!

She ducked and pushed through him. He grabbed her by the upper arm and swung her back around. She collided against his chest, gasping for breath. His hands slipped onto her sides, his face an inch from hers. She froze, her brain flashing back to that moment when they'd come so close to kissing.

"If you leave, I'll miss you," he teased.

Her jaw clenched. "Go—"

Someone banged on the door, and Sandstorm's head jerked in the direction of the noise.

Juliet shoved her hand into his chest which fragmented around her like he wasn't even there. Undeterred, she swiveled her hand in a circle, throwing off a blast of power that spiraled out and knocked him in multiple directions at once. His particles scattered to the corners of the room. She yanked one of the teleportation disks out of her pocket and hit the button.

He reformed on the other side of the room, staring at her. The blue light of the portal exploded between them. Juliet dove through.

Chapter Seventeen

Juliet stumbled into an empty parking garage as the lights flickered around her. She faced the portal, praying Sandstorm wouldn't pop through. The blue light shone for a moment then went out, leaving her alone.

She swallowed as she put the disk back in her pocket. Had she really escaped? Where was she?

They could come after me. I need to move.

Not wanting to run barefoot, she kicked off the ground and hovered through the mostly empty garage towards the exit. She burst out into the street. A purple and pink sky filled with puffball clouds greeted her.

I missed you, sky, and man, I missed flying.

She zoomed into the air above the traffic which was steady but not full-on rush hour jam-packed. A few cars honked at her, but she ignored them, stopping to hover a little over the nearest building to get a sense of her surroundings. Her heart lightened. She was only a few blocks from DOSA's local HQ.

Indulging in a full loop-the-loop followed by a barrel roll, she sped towards HQ.

She landed in front of it and hurried to the glass doors. There was a security panel with a place to swipe an ID card. She pushed the "call" button.

One of her teammates, Kesia, strode into the lobby and her mouth dropped open. Her voice didn't carry through the glass, but from the way she was waving her arms and how wide-open her mouth was, she had to be screaming. Several more people rushed into the lobby, one of whom sent relief flooding through her.

Her heart rocketed into her mouth, and she banged on the door, jumping up and down to get Shawn's attention.

He rushed to her, hit the button to open the doors, and tackled her in a hug.

"Shawn!" she gasped.

Juliet hid her face against her brother's shoulder, accepting his rib-cracking embrace.

"Are you all right?" she stammered.

He pulled away to arm's length. "Am *I* all right? Jules, you just escaped a gang of supervillains." He brushed his hand down her cheek. "They didn't ... are you okay?"

"I'm fine, but—" She glanced at the other DOSA agents, all of whom stood a respectful distance back, before dropping her voice to a whisper. "I know they were trying to get to you. Did they—the ... what you sent?"

Realization lit Shawn's eyes. "It was a dummy pack. Committee chief Talon has experts who can put together out-of-date and altered files that'll fool most supervillains into thinking they're getting real intelligence even if all of it is either useless or misleading. It's okay. I'm okay. I'm just glad you're safe."

He drew her in for another hug as her legs gave out. She was safe, and Shawn hadn't lost everything.

"Thank God. Just thank God." He closed his eyes and hid his face in her hair. "It's a miracle."

Warmth spread through her. Yeah, it kind of was.

"How'd you get away?" Pangolin came up behind Shawn followed by Kesia and Donny.

"It's a long story." Juliet pried herself away from Shawn and wiped at her eyes. "We're in trouble, though. The villains who took me have more bombs planted all around the city. They're going to use them in some sort of extortion plan."

"Do you know where?" Pangolin asked.

Regret stung her conscience. "I'm sorry, no. I overheard their plans, but not the details. We have to act fast, though. They know we're onto them, so they might just set off the devices and cut their losses. They're ...

they're not good people."

"Yeah, that's the definition of villain." Kesia snorted.

"We know where they had the first two, though, so we have an idea of the sort of locations they're targeting," Pangolin said. "It's a large enough search area that we'll need normie law enforcement—"

Everyone's phones went off simultaneously.

The group exchanged glances before all four sables, except the phone-deprived Juliet, pulled out their cellphones.

Pangolin's jaw dropped. "What the heck—"

Juliet looked over Shawn's shoulder.

A message flashed on the phone: **We have planted multiple bombs in undisclosed locations. Want to save your city? Click on the link and authorize access to your financial accounts. If enough citizens donate, no one has to die. Think of the children.**

As added insult, the text message ended with a winky face before the link.

"We're too late." Juliet's shoulders slumped. Innocent but panicked people would be giving every red cent to stop this—or if they didn't, if people assumed it was a hoax or didn't want to give enough funds to satisfy the villains, people would die. Either way, lives would be ruined.

"We need to stop this," Donny stammered.

"You think?" Pangolin's phone vibrated, flashing with an incoming call. "Crap. It's committee chief Talon. What am I going to tell him?" He held up a finger to silence those around him.

Juliet gripped Shawn's hand. Why hadn't she got those bomb locations? She should've tried harder.

"Yes, chief, we saw it ... yeah, my team's here. Uh ... Park?" Pangolin glanced at Juliet and Shawn. "Which one? ... Yeah, we have Zest back. It's a long story, and we don't have time ... Speaker? I guess." Pangolin held the phone a little ways from his face, switching to the speaker.

"Juliet Park?" a deep voice echoed from the phone.

"Yes," Juliet said hesitantly.

"You escaped or they let you go?"

She stood straighter. "Escaped, sir."

"Good work. Look, this is ... this is hard to explain, but the gang that had you, we had a long-term undercover asset planted among them. Unfortunately, we lost contact some time ago. We thought he might've been compromised, but recently your brother received a communication suggesting he was still active."

Cold washed through Juliet. "An undercover agent?"

"Yes, his name is Jake Lucas."

Lucas ...

Juliet's knees went wobbly. "I ... he's there."

"Do you have any way to reach him?"

The disk!

She reached into her pocket, but as she did, her hand brushed up against something else, something hard, small, and rectangular. What ...

She pulled out a thumb drive. "Oh—" She held it up. "I didn't ... I think he gave me this."

Her mind flitted back to when she'd last seen Sandstorm. He'd had a thumb drive, but how had it gotten into her pocket? During the fight? Yeah, he probably could've planted it on her during that.

Kesia snatched it from her. "Got it. I'll see what's on here." She ran to the nearby desk in the lobby and turned on the computer station that was there.

Juliet's insides quivered. *Undercover agent ... does that mean ...*

The pieces fell together, how careless he'd been with the security codes around her, how he'd left her with access to tools and even potential weapons, how loose-lipped he'd been. He'd *wanted* her to escape. Had he even thrown their last fight?

Oh, Sandy.

Shawn glanced down at her and mouthed, "Are you okay?"

She shook her head.

"Got it!" Kesia crowed. "Boss, it's a map with locations marked out. Looks like four of them."

"We've got this," Pangolin said. "Park, you want to come with?"

Juliet opened her mouth before following his eye line and realizing he was addressing Shawn.

"Do you need me? I want to stay with my sister," Shawn said.

"Nah, we've got enough manpower to take these down. Hopefully DOSA's tech teams can block the financial transfers." Worry flooded Pangolin's face. "Committee chief?"

"Our best techs are already working on it. Can you give me to Miss Park?"

"Yes, of course." Pangolin passed her the phone then motioned to the remainder of his team. They took off running.

"He ... he's undercover?" Juliet asked. "One of us?"

"It's a long story, but yes. Do you know where their hideout is? Maybe we can get a team to extract him."

"I don't. They used teleportation disks to get in and out, and I never saw the outside of the lair." She reached into her pocket, her hand encircling the disk. "I have one of their disks, though. It ... it can take us back."

Talon let out a breath. "Unfortunately, I can't afford to pull Pangolin's team off their current mission. It's possible he's not compromised yet and still has some time. I'll get a group to you as quickly as I can. Excuse me, I need to make a call." The phone went silent.

Juliet stared blankly at it.

"You know this agent?" Shawn murmured.

"Not as well as I thought, apparently," Juliet whispered.

"It's rough, but ... that sort of work is risky." Shawn cleared his throat. "He could still be okay. Do you have a reason to believe they're onto him?"

Juliet balled her hands into fists. Diamondback had already tried to kill Sandstorm, and her escape would only give him more reason to turn on his teammate. Wallace might keep him alive, but if their bomb plot fell through—and with DOSA having the intel Sandstorm had provided, it definitely would—they'd want to know why. What if they saw the feeds of Sandstorm downloading the information from the computer? Would they put it together? Would they ... what would they do to him?

"This isn't right!" she stammered. "DOSA can't leave him there."

"Jules, he's only one agent." Shawn gripped her shoulders. "There are multiple doomsday devices planted around this city right now, threatening thousands of lives, and a financial scheme that could wipe out the livelihoods of every single citizen if we don't stop it. There's no way DOSA can prioritize a single agent over all that."

Her mind flashed back to when Sandstorm had been injured by Diamondback, what he'd said to her.

I'm not afraid to die ... but I don't want to die alone.

How could he be any more alone than he was right now? Surrounded by false teammates who would turn on him when they discovered his secret? Abandoned by the agency that should protect him?

Oh, and the last things I said to him. The terrible, terrible things I said to him.

She pulled one of the portal disks out of her pocket. "I need to go back for him! If DOSA won't save him, I have to!"

"Heck no!" Shawn's hand shot out and snatched the disk from her.

Juliet gaped at him as he tucked it into his back pocket. "I almost lost you because you made a stupid, impulsive decision and ran in on your own without backup. I am *not* letting you do it again."

"Give that back!" she snarled.

"No." He took a step away from her. "Look, you're staying here, but I'll see what I can do. I'm not going to risk going after him on my own. I want to see my kids grow up, you know? But if I can get a few more heroes in here, I'll lead a team. I'm going to call Talon and see what resources he can get me." He held up a finger in front of her face. "Stay here. You almost broke Mom and Dad's hearts, Jules. I am not letting you throw yourself into a pit of vipers to save some random dude."

Juliet opened her mouth to yell at him, but then her hand strayed back to her pocket and the second portal disk. The one he didn't know she had.

He stared her down. "Are we clear?"

"Crystal," she said simply.

He nodded before walking away, already dialing his phone. Juliet waited until he was on the other side of the room to pull out the second disk and hit the activation button. The blue light flashed. Shawn gave a shout, but she ignored him and jumped through.

Chapter Eighteen

Sandstorm's being broke apart with a burst of pain, like somehow getting punched a million times at a microscopic level. His breath left him as he found himself exploding outward in a cloud then rushing back together with disorienting speed. He hit his knees as Juliet Park jumped through the portal, and it disappeared behind her.

Relief rushed through him. She was safe. She was finally safe. He gingerly picked himself up.

The pounding on the door behind him increased in intensity.

"Lucas! Lucas, are you in there? What's going on?"

Wallace. Well, this'll be fun to explain.

"Hold on!" he rasped. "I ... I'm coming." He limped to the door and unlocked it. Wallace and Diamondback immediately burst through. He looked around. "Where's Mentallica?"

"Found her tied up in your girlfriend's room," Diamondback answered. "Left her there to stew, but she's fine." He scanned the room, craning his neck to see over Sandstorm's shoulder as if Juliet might be hiding behind him. "You let the girl get away, didn't you?"

Sandstorm huffed. "*Let,* no. Took a beat down from before she escaped, yes."

He rubbed the back of his neck. Yeah, he'd known the importance of making that look real, but dang, did she have to hit that hard? Well, as far as she was concerned, it *had* been real. Not her fault she'd acted on that.

He shook himself out of it. "I'm going to make sure Mentallica is okay—"

Wallace snapped her fingers, and the door slammed

shut in his face. He swallowed and turned to face her.

"Explain how the DOSA agent got away," Wallace said coldly.

Sandstorm held up his hands. "Look, I did what I could to keep her from escaping. You can watch the tapes back if you doubt me, but considering the fact that she also overcame Mentallica, it's obvious we all underestimated her. I'll take responsibility for my part in that, but it's only a part."

"Or you let her go because you're a traitor," Diamondback said.

"I'm not the one who left my teammate tied up," Sandstorm pointed out. "We don't have time for infighting. She took a teleportation disk with her. If she hands that over to DOSA they could use it to infiltrate this lair. We need to bug out—"

Diamondback's jaw dropped. "You want to cut and run? What about the mission?"

"Huxley's right." Wallace shook her head. "We put everything into this plan. If we abandon it, we'll have nothing. That's not an option, but the opposite is. We're going to have to accelerate the timetable to now."

A chill cut through Sandstorm. "Are we ready?"

"Huxley, go get Mentallica. She'll get things started," Wallace said. "With the threat of our plan looming over them, DOSA won't have time to deal with us. Also, the financial transfers will all be going into an offshore account. Once we've set things up, we can port out and regroup later but still collect our funds."

A grin crossed Diamondback's face. "Finally. Payday." He hurried off.

Sandstorm's brain scrambled. This was happening too fast. DOSA wouldn't have time to act on the information he'd given Juliet, even assuming she'd found it and figured out what it was. He needed to buy time.

"I still think we need to run," he said. "Even if everything goes according to plan, DOSA could get a second team together to send through while they deal with the bombs. We can't handle an assault from a full DOSA team right now."

"We won't have to. After all, we can still leave. Like I said, we can access the funds remotely, so as soon as that's started we just need to let it run."

"The funds, yes," Sandstorm said. "But not the devices. Those were intentionally set up so they can only be armed or disarmed from the command center or in person. Are we going to bluff? Say we're going to set them off then not? Even if they don't pay up?"

He could work with that. The financial loss would be hard on anyone who paid the extortion fees, but at least no one would die.

"No, if the bombs aren't a real threat we'll lose any leverage on future heists, and I will want to replicate this if it goes well. Maybe take it to larger cities or even hold the whole country hostage." Wallace's eyes glinted. "We'll put the bombs on a timer, to go off in half-hour increments. After the first goes off, people will rush to give us everything to stop the second from also detonating. It'll increase our yield, and if we let it run down the timers, we won't need to be here. After all, the only reason we'd need to get to them is to stop them from going off, and I'm fine if they do."

Sandstorm's heart splashed into his stomach. "Wallace, that'll kill thousands of people."

"Oh, it will." A cold smile crept across her thin lips. "What's the record for deaths attributed to a single supervillain team? A few hundred? I'll rocket past that into the record books and do so while making a profit." She clapped Sandstorm on the shoulder. "And you'll be right there with me, Lucas. Your uncle would be proud."

"Yeah, I guess he would," Sandstorm mumbled.

"I'm going to arm the bombs. I think a half hour before the first detonation then one following every thirty minutes or so should do nicely—" She left the room, headed for the command center.

Sandstorm tried to clear his head. He had to stop this, but how? Ideally DOSA would be able to find and disarm the devices before they went off, but he couldn't count on that. Even with the intel he'd provided, they were scattered throughout the city, and with Wallace's new plan, they only had a half hour until the first detonated. That wasn't enough time.

I can disable the countdowns once they're set, but if any of the others notice, they'll just restart them. I'd need to disable them and then make sure they can't be re-enabled.

Taking advantage of a few minutes alone, he opened up their supply drawers and rummaged through. *Disruptor cuffs, teleportation disks ... ah, there we go.*

He pulled out a case of breacher strips, low-grade explosives meant to blast open doors. They used them for entries on smash-and-grab heists. Not enough of a yield to do much damage, but strapped to a computer, yeah, they'd do the trick. He took out one package of them along with the detonator. These worked with a remote. He hid them under his jacket and strolled down the hallway.

Mentallica, looking irritable and with some weird, orangish stain all over the back of her T-shirt, crouched over one of the computers, typing something out. Wallace stood over her, watching.

"I've hacked into the emergency broadcast system, so once this gets started, it should pop up on every device that can receive those alerts," Mentallica was explaining. "Are we ready?"

Wallace sat before the other station, looking over the program that controlled the detonation sequence. "Yeah, we're good." She turned and eyed him. "I told Diamondback to prep for the evacuation. You should as well. We can't take much, but make sure you have supplies. It might be a few days until we can regroup and claim our funds, so we need to be prepared to live off the grid."

"Gotcha." Sandstorm left but instead of heading down to the quarters level took the ladder up to the section above. Accessing his powers so he could hover weightlessly over the floor and no one would hear his footsteps, he moved to the vent above the command center.

"Okay, the extortion program is starting. If it works, we should see funds transferred into the account soon," Mentallica said. "I'm not sure I understand how this is going to work with the bombs, though. If we're evacuating, how are we going to be here to control them?"

"Do your work, and I'll take care of that," Wallace mumbled.

Contempt rippled through Sandstorm. She wasn't going to tell Mentallica they were about to commit mass murder. Typical.

Mentallica stood. "All right. That's done. What now?"

"Now we pack." Wallace cracked her knuckles. "If you hurry, you'll have time for a shower before we have to leave. You smell like a school lunchroom."

"Tell me about it—" The two women left the command center, closing and from the clicks, locking the door behind them.

Sandstorm took a deep breath. Once this was done, he'd have limited time. Best case scenario, disable the programs, destroy the computers, get to the teleportation disks, and get out before they caught him.

Okay, God, I asked if You could get me through this. Well, this is the this I was talking about. Let's go.

Fragmenting, he poured himself through the vent into the command center. Bombs first. Wallace hadn't even locked the computer—not that it would've mattered. He knew the passcodes. The program displaying the various countdowns displayed on the screen, the numbers flicking down second by second.

Sandstorm toggled off the detonations then turned his attention to Mentallica's station. She had locked hers. He unlocked it and pulled up her program. Was there an option to disable and reverse the transfers? Nope—just an execute and a kill program. Well, hopefully they hadn't stolen too much from people already. He chose the kill command before taking out the breacher strips and running them across both computer stations. He then faded through the wall into the hallway and hit the button on the detonator remote.

A boom shook the floor and rattled the walls. Smoke billowed from the door and surrounded him. He coughed and waved it away, pulling up his T-shirt collar to cover his mouth and nose. He made his way to the door which now hung off its hinges. Blinking his watery eyes, he managed to get a view of the computers. They looked toasted.

Good work. Now to get out of here—

An invisible force slammed him through the doorway and against the wall. He landed hard, the world swimming.

"I should've known," Wallace's voice pierced his confusion.

He opened his eyes, fumbling for his powers, but before he could, something metal flew through the air and fastened around his neck like a collar. His powers fizzled out. His vision cleared.

Wallace hovered in the doorway, her face twisted in rage.

"Boss, what's going on? What was that—" Mentallica rushed up behind Wallace then stopped dead, staring at Sandstorm and the chaos surrounding him.

He got to his feet and clawed at the disruptor cuff strapped around his neck.

"Dude, what blew up?" Diamondback appeared in the doorway next to the women. His eyes clouded over then lit up. "Well, well, Sand Rat. What did you do?"

Sandstorm searched for a lie that could cover for this somehow. The furious expressions of his former teammates and the prickling of Mentallica's powers rummaging through his thoughts put that idea to rest.

It's over.

His mind stayed alert, but something in his spirit gave, like a muscle clenched so long he'd forgotten what it had felt to relax.

No more lies. I don't have to lie anymore.

Mentallica stepped forward, eyes on fire. "I was always impressed by how you kept our team one step ahead of DOSA. How when every other Black Fox cell was fighting to survive, ours always managed to come out on top, escaping with plenty of breathing room, completing our missions before the good guys showed up. I always thought you were some sort of mad genius, but it wasn't that, was it? You knew when they were coming, didn't you?"

Sandstorm stayed silent. He focused on drawing his powers into the sections of his body not touching the disruptor cuff itself. He managed to get his limbs to fragment once more. He'd kept that trick of his powers to himself during his time with the Black Foxes. Maybe he could use it to his advantage and somehow get out of this.

"You've been playing our whole gang for suckers for two years now!" Diamondback hissed.

Sandstorm indulged in a smile. If it really was over, might as well enjoy what little was left. "Nah, it's been much longer than that."

"I trusted you." Mentallica's voice wavered, and Sandstorm's eyes cut to her.

Oh crap, is she tearing up?

"It was a good con, and you played it for a while, but it's over," Wallace said. "Take him down, but keep him alive for now. I want to find out how long he's been compromised and what he's fed to DOSA."

Diamondback cracked his knuckles. "Gladly. For once the coward will have to take the hits."

Diamondback strode forward. Sandstorm ducked and dodged. Diamondback grabbed his arm, but sank through it, stumbling into the wrecked computers. Knowing he couldn't go through the wall with the parts of his body touching the disruptor still solid, Sandstorm bolted for the door.

Wallace swiped her hand at him, hitting the solid sections of his body and sending him flying into the door frame.

"Mentallica!" Wallace snapped.

The younger woman darted forward and grabbed him by the shoulder. The numbing, tingling power of her sleep ability rushed through him and all went black.

Chapter Nineteen

Sandstorm's head lolled forward against his chest. An irritating energy hummed against his neck and core. Instinctively he reached for his powers only to have them die out.

"He twitched. Is he up?" Diamondback's voice jerked him back to the present, filling his head with a mix of panic and memory.

His eyes opened, letting harsh light flood in, and he tried to leap to his feet only to find himself bound. His vision cleared.

He was sitting in one of the storage rooms on the lair's middle level, his body strapped to a chair. A second disruptor cuff had been secured around him, this one across his chest and arms, further preventing him from using his powers. Wallace, Diamondback, and Mentallica stood over him.

"Yeah, he's up." Mentallica approached. "You want me to read him?"

"Do what you can, but we're running out of time," Wallace said.

"This'll be fun." Diamondback leaned against the door frame.

Mentallica clamped her hand on Sandstorm's forehead, and the prickling sensation of her powers prying at his thoughts overwhelmed his brain. He winced.

"I'm in his head," Mentallica said. "Ask what you want."

"How long have you been working with DOSA?" Wallace asked.

Sandstorm focused on his surroundings in an attempt

to think about anything but his mission. Two high metal shelves lined either side of the room, crowded with cleaning supplies, toilet paper, and other miscellaneous items. To his chagrin, a disruptor remote sat on one of the nearest shelves, next to another set of spare disruptor cuffs and some of the same cording that was now holding him to the chair. Taunting him just out of reach.

No, don't try to distract yourself. Tell us about your mission, Mentallica said in his head.

"There's nothing to tell," he said aloud instead. "It's over."

"Does DOSA know our location?" Wallace asked.

He shrugged, or at least the closest approximation he could get to a shrug with his arms bound tight to his side and his back pressed against the chair. "Who am I to say what DOSA knows? I don't even know what I know most days."

"Being a smartass isn't going to get you out of this," Mentallica said.

"Is anything going to get me out of this?" he asked calmly.

To his surprise, Mentallica flinched.

"Maybe he'll talk if I break his fingers." Diamondback slid forward, fangs bared. "Can I, boss?"

Sandstorm stiffened. Yeah, he didn't expect to make it out of this alive, but he also wasn't eager to be tortured.

Wallace checked her phone. "No. We can't know for sure that DOSA wasn't tracking him somehow, and if they were, they could show up at any minute. The time it would take to break him down through those methods—well, it's time we simply don't have." She slipped her phone into a leather case attached to her belt. "We need to cut our losses, tie up our loose ends, and move out."

Relief over the lack of torture flooded through him only to be immediately followed by dread. He was one of those loose ends, and he knew how this was going to end. His fingers twitched, longing for the bottle cap in his pocket. It always grounded him to a moment, a time he hadn't allowed himself to think of in years. He fought through the despair and panic to find it again. His father's face, worried but proud. His mother's embrace, her tears, but her acceptance that he'd made his choice. Her voice echoed in his mind.

Never forget who you are, not by birth, but because of who loves you, who chose you.

He closed his eyes. She'd had so much faith that he'd make it through this alive and come home. This was going to hurt her and Dad so much.

I didn't forget, Mom. My name is Jake Powell. Your son. I stayed on the path. I promise. It was a fight, but I kept my soul, and I'm so sorry I can't say goodbye. I wish I could just say goodbye.

"What's he thinking?" Diamondback snickered. "Is he about to piss himself?"

"Close," Mentallica answered. "He's crying for his mommy ... I thought she was dead."

"Long story." Jake opened his eyes. "You going to get this over with?"

Maybe he couldn't even have the dignity of his own private thoughts in this moment, but he wasn't going to go down begging. He had nothing to be ashamed of. He'd done his best with the life he'd had. A few more years would've been nice, a chance to have a family of his own, to live a normal life as himself, with his loved ones, with ... with her.

Though he knew the futility of it, he held Juliet's face in his mind's eyes one more time. Remembering the spark in her dark eyes, the ferocity but also mischief that so often played about her mouth, how warm and real she'd felt that one time he'd allowed himself to hold her. A hunger grew within him, cracking his resolve.

Dear God, let her find out that I'm not ... I'm not what she thinks. Please, I don't want to be a monster in her memory. Even if I had to be. Please, let my parents be okay. I'll see them again, right? That was the promise. If so, I'm ready. Just ... please, if this could not hurt a ton, that'd be cool.

He'd never been great at praying. What he wouldn't do for his mom's words right now?

Knowing he couldn't reach his parents, he tried to focus on keeping himself calm but found his thoughts instead turning once more to Juliet.

Man, he had it bad.

Kind of dumb to find someone who made him feel like she did right before the end. A bit of a waste, but for all he knew she would've rejected him anyway. After all, he'd kidnapped her, held her hostage, and blackmailed her beloved brother.

Yeah, I wouldn't have had a shot with her, and I wouldn't have deserved one. Still... If I have to die now, might as well do it in love.

Jake stopped fighting the hunger but instead savored it, allowed the longing to flow through him and consume him, allowed himself the indulgence of every memory, every little stolen moment where she'd made him feel human again with a life outside of the mission.

What would it have been like? To tell her? To open himself up and give her all his secrets? It would've gotten them both killed, but now, with his death looming, it was his one regret. As impossible as it was, he would've liked a chance to tell her the truth, to tell her he'd fallen in love with her.

"Why are we waiting?" Diamondback's irritating voice interrupted his thoughts.

Jake glanced at him. Diamondback moved with a nervous energy, like a kid who had been sitting at his desk too long and could see the clock ticking down to recess.

Contempt welled up in Jake.

"You're going to enjoy this, aren't you?" He scowled. "You psycho."

"Yeah, I am." Diamondback bared his fangs. "Come on, Wallace. Let me dose him."

"No." Wallace stepped forward.

Diamondback's face fell.

Jake tensed. Was he going to get a reprieve somehow? That seemed unlikely. His heart sank again when Wallace passed Mentallica a switchblade.

"We're compromised. We don't know how much he leaked to DOSA before we caught him, but we have to prepare for the worst, which means we need to ditch this place and find a clean lair. Huxley's method takes too long, and he's already survived it once. Mentallica, make it quick."

Mentallica stared at the blade as if it were radioactive. "Me?"

"Like I said, I want it fast. I don't trust Huxley to do that, but you're a professional." Wallace pushed the hilt into Mentallica's hand then stepped back, opening the door. "I'm going to pack up. Have it done before I return." She left the room.

Mentallica? A cold dread washed through Jake. He'd expected Diamondback, maybe Wallace, but not—

He felt the familiar prickling feeling of her probing his brain.

Why'd you have to be a traitor? You were the only decent human being I ever met in this business and you ... you lied to me. To us!

Her outward expression didn't change, but rage and grief tainted her thoughts.

Jake focused on her eyes. *Maybe that should tell you something about the people you've chosen to ally yourself with.*

Her jaw clenched, and she moved closer, towards his exposed throat.

Yeah, play the hero card. Not all of us had that luxury. I had no chance at a DOSA life with my juvie record. No hope of being anything but what I am.

Jake's mind flashed through his own youth, through the mess his life had been before his parents had found and adopted him, but arguing with her wouldn't save him. Even if she didn't do it, the others would end him. It was inevitable, but even so, he didn't want it to be her.

I signed up to stop the Black Foxes, to keep them from hurting more people. I won't apologize for that, but ... I am truly sorry that I hurt you. Please, one last favor. Give the knife to Diamondback.

She narrowed her eyes at him. *Why? You know you aren't living through this. Why does it matter if I do it?*

Because unlike him, you have some soul left, some humanity. Don't let them take that from you. Please. You've made bad choices, but you aren't a murderer. Don't let me be the reason you become one. I know this won't save me. That's not why I'm asking. Please, though. Mentallica—Danica. Not you.

Her lower lip went slack.

"What's taking so long?" Diamondback mocked. "Lost your nerve?"

She shot Diamondback a glare before her voice returned in Jake's head.

You know if I give it to Diamondback, it won't be clean. He'll make it hurt. It's who he is, even when he doesn't hate his victims as much as he hates you.

Horrific images passed through Jake's head. He wasn't sure if they were a warning from her or his own lurid imagination, but he pushed them aside and focused on her. *I can take it.*

Her eyes searched his and their connection cut off like a breaking thread.

She faced Diamondback. "It's not fair of me to deprive you of this. You've been dreaming of it for weeks. You'll make it quick." She stared him down. "Won't you?"

He held up his hands. "All right, all right ... dead is dead after all."

Jake exhaled. Okay, this was the end. How to

prepare? Prayers done. Mentallica sorted. Nothing left but to buckle through this.

Jaw set. Eyes forward. Faith in his God sure. One last deep breath then let it come.

The wall behind Mentallica exploded.

**

Energy crackled around Juliet, and she skidded to a stop in the now empty room that she'd so recently fought Sandstorm in. The device in her hand sparked and fizzled before the portal vanished. Crap. Had the disk just burned out?

What was that smell? Smoke?

She inhaled. Yeah, smoke and something worse. Melted plastic, maybe? What had happened since she'd left and where was everyone? A box of equipment lay open nearby, so she went to see if it was anything useful. The bags inside were labeled breacher strips. She'd used those in training missions before. Might come in handy. Taking one, she shoved it into her hoodie pocket and crept out the door.

The smell strengthened as she approached the command center. Her eyes widened. The room looked like a bomb had gone off—actually that was probably literally what had happened.

Muffled voices came from one of the rooms across the hall, and she heard a door creaking open. She jumped into the command center, hovering off the floor to keep her landing soft, and hugged the wall.

"I'm going to pack up. Have it done before I return." The voice was Wallace.

Juliet's heart chilled. They were bugging out then—but have *what* done?

Juliet waited until she heard the ding of the elevator doors to peer out again. She could hear Diamondback, though the words weren't clear. At least she knew what door they were behind. Could Sandstorm be in there with them?

It's my best shot. If he's what has to 'be done' before Wallace gets back—then he's running out of time.

Juliet plotted her options. If it was Mentallica and Diamondback in there, she'd be outnumbered. She needed to go in hard or they'd take her down. Her hand strayed to her pocket with the breacher strip.

Perfect.

Setting the tape only took a moment. As soon as she hit the detonator, it ignited with a flash of fire and a cloud of smoke. Cowering slightly down the hall with her fingers in her ear, Juliet jumped to her feet. She needed to act while they were still disoriented.

Kicking off the ground she flew forward, grabbed the top of the door frame, and flipped through it, now feet first. Her bare feet collided with Diamondback's shoulders, sending him flying. He crashed into the back of the small space.

Mentallica whirled around, staring at her. Juliet dropped to the ground in a crouch and threw her hands forward, all her focus going into the strongest power blast of her life. With a yelp, Mentallica hurtled through the air, landing on top of Diamondback.

From the chair, Sandstorm gaped at her. "What are you doing here?"

"Saving you, you idiot." She fumbled in her hoodie pocket for his multi-tool. Diamondback moaned and started to pick himself up. She managed to slice through one of the cords holding Sandstorm to the chair. Would she be able to free him fast enough?

"There's a disruptor remote." Sandstorm jerked his head towards his left.

She picked it up and hit the button twice. The two disruptor cuffs fell off him. He fragmented and hopped out of the chair, leaving his bonds to fall to the floor.

"Let's go!" He yanked her towards the door only to freeze. Wallace loomed in the hallway outside, nostrils flared. Sandstorm grabbed Juliet, pulled her against him, and fragmented. Juliet gasped as the strange sensation of her molecules blending first with his and then with the floor beneath them overtook her. They sank through to the next level, landing in a crouch in the very room where she'd been held hostage mere hours before.

"We need to block the door!" Sandstorm said.

Juliet rushed to grab the wooden pallet the mattress sat on. "Will this work?"

"Yeah, probably."

Together they pulled it over, wedging it beneath the door handle.

Sandstorm did a slow turn, taking in the room. Juliet swallowed. They didn't have a lot to work with.

He faced her again. "I don't suppose you still have the teleportation disk you took?"

She shook her head. "It burned out when I ported back in."

His face fell, distress flooding his eyes. "You shouldn't have come back. I wanted you to be safe."

Her stomach quivered, and she stepped closer to him. "I couldn't leave you. I ... I just couldn't."

Something slammed against the door, and she instinctively reached for him. He drew her into an embrace, his hold tight.

"We can still fight our way out, right?" she whispered. "Two of us, three of them. We've got a chance?"

He nodded, his fingers squeezing into her upper arms. "A chance, yeah."

The door shook again. Muffled voices shouted.

"Stop banging into it like an idiot," Wallace ordered. "Go get the breacher strips."

They didn't have much time. She'd done it again. Rushed in without a thought or a plan. Not only had she failed to save him, but she'd cost him the comfort of knowing he'd saved her.

She clutched his T-shirt.

"Look, we can get through this," he said. "Stay close to

me. I'll keep you fragmented so they can't hit you, and ... we'll fight. We'll fight hard. I am not letting them take you while I'm still standing, all right?"

Her tongue stuck to the roof of her mouth. He glanced at the door. For the moment it was quiet. His hand slipped from her arm to her face, stroking her cheek. A sudden hunger overwhelmed her as their eyes met.

"Juliet, I can't ... I don't want to assume ..."

"Just ask," she breathed.

"Since this could be the end, would it be all right if I kissed you?" he murmured, bending closer.

His warm breath caressed her face, and the hunger turned into an inferno within her. She managed to nod. He leaned in, his mouth pressing against hers. Her grip on his shirt tightened as her other hand worked its way up his neck and her fingers into his soft hair. Whatever happened next, she didn't regret coming back for him. Even if it was only to die with him, she couldn't have lived with herself if she'd left him alone.

Shouts rose from outside. A woman screamed. Juliet jerked away from Sandstorm and stared at the door.

"What was that?" she stammered.

"I'm not sure." He released her except for one hand that remained on her shoulder, channeling his power into her. She was starting to like the feeling of his energy. It had a spice to it, a weird mix of revitalizing and soothing. She wished she had more time to explore what it was like, what he was like.

Something crashed outside then all fell quiet.

Sandstorm glanced at her. "What do you think—"

"Juliet?" a voice called out. Her breath left her.

"Shawn?" She ran to the door and, with Sandstorm's help, removed the pallet barrier. "Shawn!" she shouted. She emerged into the hallway. Shawn stood by the elevator with both Wallace and Diamondback at his feet, already in disruptor cuffs.

"How—" she stammered.

He held up a portal disk.

"Oh." She eyed the two villains. "There's a third."

"Upstairs. I surprised her when I ported in, and she went down easy." He shrugged. "These two put up a little bit more of a fight, but I'm kind of an old hand at this." He gave her an easy smile, though the wrinkles around his eyes betrayed his worry.

"Thank you." She started towards him.

His jaw dropped. "Look out!" He rocketed past her.

Juliet spun just in time to see one of her brother's power blasts collide with a wide-eyed Sandstorm.

"Shawn, don't!" she shrieked.

Sandstorm fragmented, but the power blast still clipped him, sending him into the wall.

"Oof!"

"Shawn, stop!" Juliet flew to her brother and grabbed his arm to stop him from aiming a punch at Sandstorm's face. "He's the undercover agent! He's DOSA."

Shawn's face fell. "Him?"

She inserted herself between them. "Yes. Him."

Sandstorm pulled himself to his feet and laughed awkwardly. "I guess we got off on the wrong foot."

"That's not even sort of covering it." Shawn frowned.

"Shawn," Juliet whispered. "It's over. I'm safe. You're safe. It's ... it's over."

His jaw clenched but then he nodded. "You're right it is." He gripped her shoulder. "Let's get out of here. Can we use the teleportation disks to take in the three prisoners?"

"Yeah, I can show you how," Sandstorm volunteered.

"Good. The sooner we're out of here the better." Shawn stalked back to where Diamondback and Wallace were bound.

Sandstorm's shoulders slumped. "He hates me."

Juliet slipped her hand into his. "He's overwhelmed. Give him some time. I mean, I hated you just a few hours ago, and I don't anymore."

He laughed. "I guess there's that. Come on. Let's get out of here."

Chapter Twenty

Juliet's head fell forward then bounced back, jerking her to full consciousness. She forced herself to sit straight again, stubbornly staring down the hospital hallway. After everything he'd gone through for her and DOSA, she could do him the favor of waiting for him even if she was—a yawn escaped her.

Dang, she was tired.

After they'd teleported the three villains back to Pittsburgh, they'd let DOSA take over. Juliet used Shawn's phone to call her parents, just to let them know she was okay, before she and Sandstorm had both been swept away to a local hospital for an evaluation. Apparently this was standard procedure after any time in enemy hands. Juliet's had been a simple list of questions and answers, but when she'd finished, Sandstorm was still in with his doctor. Rather than leave him alone at the hospital, she'd asked if she could wait for him and had been shown to a seating area.

Finally, a door opened down the hall and a doctor strode out followed by a tall, lean figure, still clad in that ridiculous leather jacket. As she watched them exchange a few words then shake hands, relief flooded through her, followed by bemusement. Between the jacket and his scuffs from the recent fighting, he certainly was leaning into the bad boy look—and he made it look good.

He caught sight of her, and his eyes lit up. She hopped out of her chair as he left the hallway and came to stand before her.

"Are you okay?" she asked, eyeing the sutures on the cut near his eye along with several smaller scrapes that appeared tended to but still had to hurt.

"Scratched up, exhausted—no permanent damage, though." He cast her one of his easy smiles, though she could tell with more effort than he was letting on. "Thanks for coming back for me."

"How could I not?" She stepped a little closer to him, longing to embrace him but not sure where they stood. Did she even know this guy at all?

He muffled a yawn with his closed fist. "Sorry. Like I said. Exhausted."

Shame flooded through her. "I shouldn't be keeping you up. This is dumb. You should be lying down, resting —"

"No, not yet." He held up his hand. "For one thing, I need to debrief. DOSA won't let me call home until I do, and I really, really want to call home." Something akin to desperation crept into his voice. "It's not even that I need to sleep, honestly. It's just, well—" He reached into his pocket and pulled out the bottle cap again, rubbing it between his fingers and thumb. "I've been on the clock for four years straight. With Mentallica around, I had to train myself to think like one of them in case she popped into my head at any given moment, so I wasn't even safe in my own brain. It really sucked."

"I bet," she murmured. "So ... your real name is Jake? Jake ... Lucas?"

"Sort of, but not really. It's a long story." He nodded towards the chairs. She sat down, and he settled beside her. "My birth name is Lucas, and yeah, my original family is made up of supervillains—or was, anyway. I think pretty much all of them are dead now, so what I said about my parents being dead and not having a family —half true. Biological family is all gone for one reason or another, mostly supervillain stuff. My adopted family, though, the ones who took me in when I was sixteen and got me off that path, they're alive and their last name— and mine too, legally—is Powell."

"Powell," she repeated. Why did that sound familiar?

A thought struck her. "You said you've been undercover for four years? Have you been able to talk to them at all?"

He grimaced. "Nope and they're probably worried sick, but they knew what I signed up for. I asked for their blessing. While they didn't like it much, they agreed it was the right thing for me to do. With my family history, I could slip into the Black Foxes in a way no one else from DOSA could. It was maybe our one chance to take the gang down from within, and like I said, it sucked, but we did it." He let out a sigh. "We finally did it."

"I can't imagine how awful that was." She rested her hand on top of his. She'd been separated from her family for not even a fraction of that time, and knowing they were worrying about her had eaten her up. What Sandstorm—Jake—had gone through was so much worse.

"Yeah." His gaze dropped to his lap then he cleared his throat. "Look, the first impression you got of me wasn't great, and I'm sorry. I promise I'm not that guy. I promise I'm ... I'm not perfect, hardly. I'm kind of messed up overall, but I got a second chance and I've tried to do right by it—"

Her eyebrows shot up. With everything she knew now, how could he think she'd think he was a bad guy? She opened her mouth, but he kept going.

"I really want a chance to start over with you, Jules—" He swallowed. "Is it okay if I call you that?"

"Please do," she whispered.

His smile returned, less forced this time. "What I'm trying to say is I'm asking for another go at a first impression, to meet you all over again, if that's all right?"

She nodded.

He stood and offered her his hand which she took, allowing him to draw her to her feet. "Hi, Juliet Park. My name is Jake Powell. I'm genetically inclined towards supervillainy, but when I was sixteen I got pulled out of it by a couple who gave me a second chance. I owe everything to them. I'm dyslexic, kind of a smart aleck, and I really like comic books and science fiction, especially *Star Wars* and *Firefly*. My parents are Fade and Lucia Powell, and I love them more than just about anything. I have two younger siblings, Ruby and Curran, but I haven't seen them in so long I doubt they remember me." A look of pain crossed his face, and she barely resisted the urge to pull him into an embrace. He closed his eyes then opened them again, their hazel depths working their way into her soul. "I am so sorry for what I put you and your family through. I was working for a good cause, but it hurt you, and I hated every moment of it. That said, I have never seen anyone as brave and resilient as you were through it all. You were so, so impressive, and ... man ... you are amazing."

Her face heated. "Not really."

"Oh, yeah, you are." He touched her face, and her insides quivered. "Maybe we could—I don't know—get to know each other a little better?"

"I'd like that." She leaned into his touch.

His smile broadened, and he bent closer, bringing his lips to hers. Her arms slipped around him, and she held on for dear life as his mouth moved against hers until nothing mattered but his warmth. A floodgate opened, and Juliet relaxed into it, parting her lips so that his tongue could meet hers, ever so slightly. Her fingers found their way into his hair, and his hold on her tightened. She closed her eyes and allowed him to fully support her, savoring the strength of his arms and the gentleness of his hands and ...

Jake went rigid then jerked away. She opened her eyes and found him staring past her. A chill crept through her and she turned around.

Dave Park's eyes expanded like a cartoon character's.

"Dad!" Juliet gasped as Jake released her. "Where ... uh ..."

"Mr. Park?" Jake said hesitantly.

"Yes, that's my name." Her father came closer and

embraced her for a long moment. "I'm so glad you're safe."

Pushing aside the embarrassment of being caught mid-PDA, Juliet hugged him back. "I'm glad I am too. I missed you so much."

Her dad kissed her forehead then released her and eyed Jake from top to bottom. The tall young man stood a little straighter, towering several inches over Dad, but still looking intimidated.

"I was told that Juliet came up here to check on the undercover agent who saved her life during her recent captivity," her father explained. "I'm assuming that's you?"

"I guess." Jake laughed uncomfortably. "To be honest, I pulled her into the whole mess in the first place, but it was an accident. I'm sorry for the worry I must've caused you and your family."

"It wasn't pleasant, but from what Pangolin has told me, she wouldn't have made it home if not for you." Her dad nodded slowly. "He was uncertain about several details. Including your name. He thought it might be Lucas? Is that correct."

"That's ... yes and no," Jake said. "That was my birth name. I was adopted by a couple who run a camp for at-risk superpowered teens and legally took their last name. I only used my birth name during the mission because it made it easier to get into the Black Foxes."

"Camp for superpowered—" Realization flooded Dad's face. "The SVR? You're a Powell then?"

"Yes, well, not by birth, but they're my family." Jake smiled.

"In my experience with that clan, its members are as often chosen by the family as they are born into it. Good people."

"Yeah, they are." Jake's voice sank to a murmur before he raised his eyes to meet her father's again. "I do want to apologize, sir, for the pain I know I put you and your family through. It was all for the good of the mission, but it still wasn't right. I'm sorry, and if there's anything I can do to make it up to you, please, let me know."

Her father looked past Jake, seeking Juliet. For some reason, she couldn't hold his stare.

"Based on what I saw when I walked in on you, it seems my daughter has already forgiven you, and if she's safe and well that's all that matters," he said.

Juliet rested her hand on Jake's shoulder. "I have."

The relief and happiness that spread across Jake's face warmed her heart.

"In fact, considering she came home safe to me when the results could've been far worse, I feel in some way I owe *you* a debt," her dad continued. "Perhaps dinner? On me?"

"That is a generous offer, but I was kind of hoping I could take your daughter out tonight, just the two of us." Jake's eyes twinkled. "If that's all right?"

Something fluttered in Juliet's chest.

"Even better." Dave offered Jake his hand. "I hope this won't be the last time we talk, Jake Powell."

"Something tells me it won't be," Jake addressed her father, shaking his hand, but kept his eyes firmly on Juliet. Her cheeks caught fire.

Dave nodded to his daughter before walking away.

Juliet turned towards Jake. "Dinner, huh? Funny you haven't asked me yet."

"Yeah, well, that's because I forgot to mention, all my assets are currently tied up in a DOSA investigation, so I essentially don't have a red cent to my name." He smirked. "If we go out, you're treating."

"I hope you like McDonald's then, Sandy," she scoffed.

His eyes sparkled. "Perfect. I could use a good cheeseburger. It's a date, then?"

"It's a date." She squeezed his hand. They stood in

silence for a long moment, his eyes taking her in in a way that made her whole being feel lighter.

"I still need to debrief," he finally said. "Another reason I turned your dad down is because DOSA wants me to hop on a bird to DC to report directly to Committee Chief Talon. I asked if I could fly you in with me, and they said that it could be arranged, but I don't think I could get permission for another passenger on short notice."

"Oh." She glanced down at her sweatshirt. "I'm not exactly dressed to go to DC HQ."

He laughed. "They'll give you a chance to change first, I'm sure. We have a couple hours. Though maybe I can get Talon to loan me fifty bucks so you won't have to pay for dinner."

She snorted. "Do you get loans from the committee chief often?"

"After what I went through for DOSA, I feel like money for dinner is a pretty small ask." He nodded towards the exit. "The doctor said there would be a car waiting for me. Ready to go?"

She nodded. "Definitely."

Wherever this was headed, it was going to be amazing.

The End

ABOUT H. L. Burke

Born in a small town in north central Oregon, H. L. Burke spent most of her childhood around trees and farm animals and always accompanied by a book. Growing up with epic heroes from Middle Earth and Narnia keeping her company, she also became an incurable romantic.

An addictive personality, she jumped from one fandom to another, being at times completely obsessed with various books, movies, or television series (Lord of the Rings, Star Wars, and Star Trek all took their turns), but she has grown to be what she considers a well-rounded connoisseur of geek culture.

Married to her high school crush who is now a US Marine, she has moved multiple times in her adult life but believes home is wherever her husband, two daughters, and pets are.

For information about H. L. Burke's latest novels, to sign up for the author's monthly newsletter, or to contact the writer, go to:

www.hlburkeauthor.com

Also by H. L. Burke

For Middle Grade Readers
Thaddeus Whiskers and the Dragon
Cora and the Nurse Dragon
Spider Spell
Absolutely True Facts of the Pacific Tree Octopus

For Young Adult Readers
An Ordinary Knight
Beggar Magic
Coiled
Spice Bringer
The Heart of the Curiosity
Ashen

The Nyssa Glass Steampunk Series:
Nyssa Glass and the Caper Crisis
Nyssa Glass and the House of Mirrors
Nyssa Glass and the Juliet Dilemma
Nyssa Glass and the Cutpurse Kid
Nyssa Glass's Clockwork Christmas
Nyssa Glass and the Electric Heart

The Dragon and the Scholar Saga (1-4)
A Fantasy Romance Series
Dragon's Curse
Dragon's Debt
Dragon's Rival
Dragon's Bride

To Court a Queen

Ice and Fate Duology
Daughter of Sun, Bride of Ice
Prince of Stars, Son of Fate

The Green Princess: A Fantasy Romance Trilogy
Book One: Flower
Book Two: Fallow
Book Three: Flourish

Spellsmith and Carver Series
Spellsmith & Carver: Magicians' Rivalry
Spellsmith & Carver: Magicians' Trial
Spellsmith & Carver: Magicians' Reckoning

Fellowship of Fantasy Anthologies
Fantastic Creatures
Hall of Heroes
Mythical Doorways
Tales of Ever After
Paws, Claws, and Magic Tales

Match Cats: Three Tails of Love

Supervillain Rehabilitation Project Universe
Relapsed (a short story prequel)
Reformed
Redeemed
Reborn
Refined

Reunion

Blind Date with a Supervillain
On the Run with a Supervillain
Captured by a Supervillain
Coming Soon: Engaged to a Supervillain

A Superhero for Christmas

Power On
Power Play
Power Through
Power Up

Made in the USA
Middletown, DE
01 June 2024